Paragon Apocrypha

A Short Story Collection of The Galvorn Saga

Mikel Melwasul
David Tullius

2025 May You Walk Under Blue Skies Publishing LLC

Paperback ISBN 978-1-968466-02-2
Hardback ISBN 978-1-968466-01-5
Ebook ISBN 978-1-968466-00-8

Edited by Megan G. Mossgrove and Mrs. Melwasul
Cover illustration by Yorsy Hernandez

1st Edition, 2025

Special thanks to K. R. Solberg for formatting
and Jon Wesley Huff for cover feedback

Special thanks to The Galvorn Saga discord
for beta reading and cover feedback.

PARAGON APOCRYPHA

A SHORT STORY COLLECTION
OF THE GALVORN SAGA

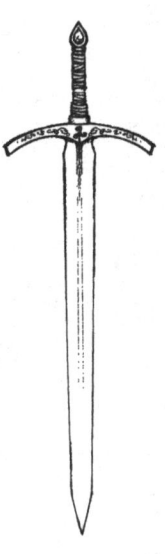

MIKEL MELWASUL
DAVID TULLIUS

This one goes out to the indie author community,
who greeted us with open arms and spare pens.

AUTHOR'S NOTE

These short stories are a little more adult than previous publications, while there is no smut some stories contain more profanity as well as some heavy topics. All stories are canonical to The Galvorn Saga universe. Some of these stories are cut chapters from old books, The Crossing is a sneak peek at Paragon Odyssey, a southern-gothic horror novella led by David, currently in development, lastly, for those of you who haven't read Paragon Exordium, we've added the Prologue as a bonus here!

Enjoy, and as always, May You Walk Under Blue Skies.

CONTENTS

$$\longmapsto 1 \longmapsto$$

MANNY THE HUMAN MAYOR

Idiot, Ohio's mayor wasn't human.

But nobody knew that.

Sure. Mayor Manny looked human: he only had one head, and all the right orifices. He didn't have a tail. He had round ears, and round pupils. He even had the standard human legs, feet, and arms. No gills, scales, or extra fur anywhere. Nothing about him was even slightly sharp.

In short, Manny was a freak.

Everyone else had tails, or gills, or six limbs, or two limbs. All the centaur children mocked him, and the mermaid children he never saw, since he only saw his mother once a year when his father took him to her lake, since he couldn't live with her.

Manny's father was a centaur, and his mother was a mermaid. So by all logic, he should have been anything but human. But magic laughs at logic. And while Manny looked as human as any human could, he wasn't. In fact, that's how he'd gotten his name. When he was born his mother asked "Don't you think that baby looks like a man?" To which his father replied: "He's a bit Manny."

He even asked his parents if they'd kidnapped him as a baby. He promised he wouldn't be mad. As far as he was concerned it would have been a perfectly normal thing to do.

But they assured him he was, in fact, their child, as unfortunate as that might be. They said he used to be more like them, but he grew out of it not long after the sky broke and the world changed. Before that, he'd lived with his mother under the lake, but he remembered none of that and wasn't sure it was true.

Every year, his father would lead the centaurs to visit that lake, and only his mother could make them drink its water for most of the centaur feared the mermaid's territory. Except for Manny's father, who'd braved it many years ago when he rescued Manny's mother from a cursed ring she'd gotten stuck around her neck.

Once Manny was grown, he set off to seek his fortune. This was odd, because it is not something centaurs or mermaids do. It was, however, something monsters believed humans did.

Eventually, he found himself in the town of Idiot, Ohio. Now it is important to note, dear reader, that Manny was stressed. He'd been stressed for as long as he could remember; almost always because of his human appearance. From not fitting in with the centaurs, or being able to swim as deep as the mermaids. But now, that stress was brought on by his fear that his interactions with humans would expose him for being not human.

So when his arrival in town coincided with a large crowd gathering, he felt like a human being in a herd of centaurs, or a human in a surge of mermaids, or really any out of place person, which was how he always felt, so, really, he felt at home.

Being mayor did nothing to help Manny's anxiety. The people of Idiot were not particularly prejudiced against non-humans. They simply had limited experience. In this regard, Manny's presence was extremely helpful in dealing with anything other than other humans. This resulted in two consecutive elections to mayoral office. So many were Manny's adventures as mayor that you could fill an entire book with them. But we are trying to keep this one short, dear reader, so we shall focus on the most important encounter of Manny's mayoral career.

During Manny's second term, a traveling massage therapist visited the town. Manny was far too nervous about the idea of a massage to get one on his own. But when the therapist showed up at his door, insisting that the service had already been paid for by members of the town who were concerned about his mental health and stress, his anxiety prevented him from rejecting her services.

It wasn't that he feared the discovery of his inhuman nature. It was more due to his lack of experience with touch. Whether that be due to centaur culture being less touch prone, or his own oddness making his fellow creatures less likely to exchange a casual hug, is a debate for another time.

Without going into excessive detail, the massage was a delightful disaster. The masseuse attacked the stress Manny manifested in his muscles with malicious merriment. Each knot knew no reprieve until it ceased to be. It was in this way that Manny discovered his human form was in fact held together by stress.

This unveiling began with the sprouting of two new arms, followed by the lengthening of his torso and the sudden appearance of scales along his sides. His feet became hooves, his ears grew points. Despite his increased relaxation resulting in increased monstrosity, the masseuse did not stop. She continued until no knots remained and embarrassment drank with relief, keeping Manny's protest at bay until there was simply no mistaking him for human.

When she was finally finished, she simply took a step back and said, "That's your time." Then departed the room without so much as a chuckle or a tease at his transformation.

When Manny woke the next morning, he was distressed to find that while he enjoyed his new form with its many limbs, odd scales, and increased height, he could not figure out how to change back. So, determined to remain professional, he sent a raven to town hall to announce an emergency town meeting.

The crowd that gathered under the cracked sky outside the upsettingly square town hall building was a chatty one. They kept their volume at a polite enough level for the mayor not to hear from where he hid just inside the building, a few steps back from the podium that awaited his resignation. He waited until enough were seated and comfortable that he was sure any missing members would get all they'd need from the local gossip column before emerging.

As he approached the podium, he expected screams, panic, maybe even insults and weapons being drawn. But, there were none; there weren't even whispers or silence. Instead, the crowd continued chattering at the same polite volume, as if it were any other mayoral announcement until he came to a stop at the now too-short-for-him podium.

The crowd quieted peacefully and, for a moment, Manny was too confused to speak. But the crowd remained silent, calm. Until a polite cough echoed from a farmer in the back, freeing him from his nervous freeze.

"Citizens of Idiot, it has been the greatest joy of my life to serve you all as your neighbor and mayor. However, due to obvious circumstances, I will be resigning my position. Effective immediately."

A gasp ran through the crowd, and an elderly crow of a lady stood and called out. "You sick? I hear there's a fairy pond a few days hike out north that'll cure just about anything."

"No, ma'am, I'm not sick. This is just what I look like."

"Then what's the obvious circumstance?" called a fat farmer.

Manny stared back at him in disbelief. Then mustered his courage to speak directly. "Well, as you can see, I am not exactly human."

"But you're not sick?" repeated the old lady.

"No, Ms. Fowl, I am not sick."

The old bat adjusted her glasses and looked down her nose at him. "If you're uncomfortable, just change back."

"I'm not uncomfortable, and I don't know how!" Manny replied, his head spinning at the dramatically unexpected reactions.

A woman with three children of various ages in her arms stood from her folded black chair. "If you don't want to be mayor Manny, that's alright. But we've known you weren't human from the day you set foot in town."

"Yeah!" Chimed in a poorly mustachioed butcher. "You're a good mayor, we don't care if you're human or not so long as you aren't about to start eating people."

The crowd chuckled good naturedly at this, and Manny felt a smile of his own clamber over his face. But he was confused, and needed clarity. "How did you already know I wasn't human?"

"You sleep standing up, exclusively," a round fellow near the back of the crowd called.

"Your head was underwater for twenty minutes during last year's apple bobbing contest!" exclaimed another voice.

"You smell like straw and seaweed!" came another declaration, which was quickly clarified. "In a good way!"

Examples went on for half an hour and left poor Manny feeling extremely embarrassed but also more cared for than he'd ever felt before.

So Manny remained mayor of Idiot, Ohio, and he's still mayor there to this day. You can stop by and see him sometime and you may find the people of that fair town not quite living up to their town's name.

That said,

Idiot, Ohio's mayor isn't human.

But everybody knows that.

SHORT TALES

Rumors are a curious thing. There isn't always a truth from which they spring. Rumors shift and wane with time, which erodes them as much as it forms them. Memories are much the same. Especially in the case of mankind. Not so for all others. To discover the story behind rumor and memory requires sifting through the sands to get to the gold. As is much the case in the following recounting. To recount another deceased human's phrase: "Truth is stranger than fiction."

How the Fellhammers, a pair of unrelated dwarves foolishly traveling across the country during the world's first and worst flood, came to speak with Russian accents is one such oddity.

The Felhammers were six and twenty days into their rain-soaked journey, moving swiftly down a stone road when the world disintegrated around them.

They'd heard a warning, a magical flair, commanding them to seek fae shelter, but they'd been nowhere near such a spot. As a result, they were not properly shielded when magic tore the them across ten millennia with a blast of bright blue light, searing pain, and the sound of the very sky being torn open.

In their defense, that was neither the intention of the spell nor a foreseen side effect. So, it comes as no surprise that when they were removed from our reality, and then, in the blink of an eye, reinserted ten thousand years later, the sensation was not a pleasant one.

When the younger of the pair woke, he found himself quite incapable of movement, a sensation made far worse by the arcane buzzing under his skin. He would later describe the sensation as "like being trapped in an electric current made of carbonation," a description as confusing as it was accurate, despite the dwarf only having been electrocuted once. The other dwarf described it as a buzzing, strangely reverberating pain, like bees shimmying through their veins.

Prior to their sudden and unexpected relocation in time, the road led up a small hill with an excellent canopy to help deal with the unending deluge. But, when they awoke to the changed world, they found themselves on an orangish dirt road amidst a scattering of pine trees, with no sign of any hill, and the sky above appearing as if it had been struck with a hammer.

Unfortunately, since both dwarves were incapable of movement, they were furthermore incapable of speech. As a result, the elder dwarf claims he decided to take a nap. However, the validity of this claim must come under some scrutiny as it is entirely possible he simply passed out from the pain.

Their secondary return to consciousness in five times as many millennia was heralded by the unfamiliar, to them, sound of an approaching truck.

Luckily enough, the pair of dwarves were not indistinguishable from a pair of logs in the road, and so the vehicle's owner came to a stop before making dwarf pancakes.

Although the pair were incapable of communication — see previous paragraphs describing their paralysis — they were capable and cognisant enough to watch as an old man emerged from his ancient truck.

Rodion was his name, but the dwarves never knew this. He was only a few degrees shy of the appearance of a vulture wearing an excellent human disguise. What little hair that did crown his head was white, whispy and exclusively to the sides and back. Yet despite his haunting visage, there was a kindness in his eyes as he peered down at the pair.

The languages he spoke, of which there were several, were unfamiliar to the dwarves. After many minutes of pacing, he proceeded to check their vitals, his face wrinkled in confusion as he got closer, the whole while repeating an odd phrase: "Cheekie Breekie."

The pain made the man's transportation too unbearable for consciousness. Despite their suffering, they were glad to be removed from the threat of exposure or predators.

When their minds retook control of their bodies, as they would put it, they found themselves no less paralyzed, but now in a strange room. Overhead, a ceiling fan sat motionless, having ended its decades-long rotation with the destruction of most of the known world. The walls were a strange, faded yellow, and the ceiling covered in oddly repeating circles of immature stalactites.

Shortly after their return to consciousness, the old man entered the room. His voice was harsh and cracky, with a kind undercurrent despite the gibberish he spoke, which both dwarves feared was a byproduct of insanity.

His speech, as confusing as it was, was animated enough to clearly meander between storytelling and lecturing the pair as he spent long hours speaking to them between spoonfuls of soup and water. He spent most of his time with them, sewing old clothes as he spoke in wandering, incomprehensible sentences. On several occasions, he pulled small paintings from a large leather tome. Odd ones, of a far off, snowy land. Many of these paintings, which we would know of as photographs, showed a much younger man in a green uniform with a red star on his chest.

Slowly, the pain dissipated from their bodies, and after two days their toes began to wiggle. At the same time, the old man sprung a cough. A cruel one that racked him from head to toe and regularly dyed his white mustache in red flecks.

Still, he cared for them, feeding them and cleaning them with wet cloth. On the evening of the last day of the first week he'd cared for them, speech returned to the elder Fellhammer, but only once the old man, now upsettingly shaky in all his movements, departed for the evening.

"Dalmack," Morind whispered in dwarvish through cracked lips. "Do you have any understanding of what's happening?"

The bushier-bearded dwarf groaned, but it wasn't until several hours later that he was able to speak. "Morind, I think we should have found proper shelter after all."

The pair of them enjoyed a joint chuckle at this before allowing themselves more rest, neither wanting to admit how taxing the short interaction was for them. The morning of the second week, Rodion collapsed, spilling food on the ground, his face as white as his usually well-manicured, curly whiskers. His un-waxed mustache hung limp, stained the color of rust. He managed to recover, much to their relief, but they were despondent at their own inability to aid him.

As the dwarves regained their strength, old man Rodion seemed to lose his. But for some reason, when he shakily woke one morning in the second week, his long-winded prattling was replaced with only the repeated words "Cheekie Breekie."

At this point, they spoke back to him in their own tongue, and his face lit up with delight, and he placed a hand on Morind and firmly said, "Cheekie." Then again, on Dalmack but this time "Breekie." All the while, smiling in a peculiar way that did not fully reach his eyes. He helped each of them sit up and fed them a gray porridge rather than just broth, all the while repeating the phrase. Then he showed them their armor, cleaned and polished, which he left on a dresser in the room for them to look at while they continued their recovery.

The third week began with him standing by their beds, where he placed clothes he'd been tailoring to better fit the dwarves. His hand lingered on each set, memories clearly tied to the old green cloth. Then he patted them softly, and whispered the same phrase. "Cheekie Breekie."

The third week ended when he carried his old body over to a rocking chair at the other end of the room, a large glass bottle in one hand. He sipped as he sat and rocked, muttering the phrase over and over, quieter and quieter. A violent cough rocked his body.

"Cheekie Breekie." The words lingered in the ears of the dwarves, tangling with the arcane energy that flowed through them. An old spell beyond their reach or comprehension at long last unravelled. With the spells breaking came arcane understanding. At long last, the dwarves knew what the odd phrase meant. The nicknames he'd given the pair meant simply "All is well."

Nothing could have been further from the truth. The old man's stroke took his last breaths as he whispered the words of comfort to the two strange dwarves he'd found in his driveway and nursed back to health.

By the time the dwarves were mobile enough to aid him, it was far too late. As they left the small guest room and explored the home, they found he'd prepared for his own demise. A long table, too tall for them to use properly, hosted travel packs full of tied foods, cantines, and a map with poorly scribbled arrows.

Tears ran into their beards as they buried Rodion in his garden. To honor him, they swore to take the names Cheekie and Breekie as their own for a time of mourning. The next day they set out. The world was changed beyond recognition, but kindness still prevailed in that old Russian man's house in south Georgia.

Or so the rumor goes.

THE SILKEN GROVE

Tarlkien didn't hate spiders, but he certainly didn't like them anymore.

He used to be indifferent; that's how he became a silk harvester. But after hundreds and hundreds of trips into the Silken Grove, his ambivalence was shifting. Little spiders were still fine, easy enough to squash to not be a bother.

But the spiders of the silken grove ranged in size from bobcat to griffin. He'd even heard that the queen was the size of a dragon. He shivered at the thought as he pulled on his magic nonstick-boots, and donned his special goggles — one of ten pairs in existence. The original design was dwarvish, for mining dangerous crystal formations that emitted a strong light, but the elves had modified the design for spider silk. The goggles filtered the effects of the millions of webs in the grove which wreaked havoc on elvish vision. Without them, their enhanced vision would be overwhelmed by the kaleidoscopic effect of the millions of tiny shiny strings.

I wonder if she moves as silently as the rest. I certainly hope not, but none of them ever make a sound until they're about to strike.

Luckily for him, the queen wasn't his responsibility. He rarely ventured far into the grove, instead tasked with collecting the silk the elves harvested for armor and all other manner of industry from around the edges of the contained Forest.

He had two primary tasks: collecting silk, and making sure the moonlight lanterns around the perimeter stayed lit.

He was halfway through his route, too far to simply turn back, when he heard a familiar creaking noise.

Tarlkien froze. Gnarsh is here. *What drives a dryad to take on such a form?* The other attendees refused to talk about Gnarsh other than vague whispers.

The Dryads, tree spirits, usually took humanoid shape rolling from the wood of their chosen tree.

But Gnarsh cared as much for the spiders as he did for the trees of the Silken Grove. This was demonstrated by his form — an elvish upper body, growing out of a spider abdomen with spindly, creaking legs. The elvish part of his form was meant to provide comfort, or at least a false sense of familiarity. But its nudity, bald head, and extra eyes and arms had the opposite effect.

Tarlkien turned slowly and looked up to see the creature hanging upside down above him from a long web, his form being entirely wooden added to his strangeness.

"She has taken Yalvana," Gnarsh chittered in speech barely decipherable as elvish.

A bolt of fear stabbed into Tarlkien's chest. "Who?" Yalvana was the Warden of the Silken Grove. The oldest elf he'd ever met. She was the first to weave spidersilk into armor. Yalvana was a living legend, but she could only mean one thing. The queen.

"Follow." The simple word made his heart drop into his stomach.

I should get help. There was no time. Gnarsh was already moving; if he lost track of him now there was no guarantee the creature would seek help again. *What if he's lying?* The possibility left a weight in his gut. The dryad wasn't right in the head already; what if his odd sense of being meant he was curious what elf tasted like?

Tarlkien drew his thin, curved short sword. It was more a tool than a weapon, but what were weapons if not tools for killing? Probably better than his blade for harvesting silk.

Still. The forest floor was soft. Usually elvish footsteps were too light to generate sound or disturb the ground, but here, among the hidden webs even the lightest step could alert danger. He was dressed to compensate for this: his clothes were web resistant, his boots were enchanted to keep him from signaling any spiders when he stepped on their webs. Despite this, he held his breath.

The deeper he got into the dark trees, the thicker the webs grew. He slipped his goggles on to help with the dwindling light. For a moment, he wished he had human vision rather than the sharp eyes of an elf. He could see them. Hundreds of them in the branches all around him. Thousands of eyes. Hungry eyes. Watching with malicious intent, waiting for his steps to catch in a web, for him to stumble and become further tangled.

They were fed two days ago, he reminded himself. *Most shouldn't be hungry again for a while.* But the sound of clicking mandibles in the dark dissuaded the thought that full stomachs would turn them from violence.

He wondered if they would swarm him and tear him to shreds, or if one of the bigger ones would win out, driving the others back before filling his veins with venom and eating him inch by inch, leaving him paralyzed and unable to scream as each piece of him was torn away by mandibles.

I shouldn't have come, he thought, as he followed Gnarsh around a hollow tree, sword raised in anticipation of what waited on the other side. *Yalvana can take care of herself. She practically grew the grove on her own.* But he knew that wasn't true. Yalvana was behind it, yes, but no elf could have done all this alone. Worse, Yalvana was kind. To abandon her would not only be immoral, it would be cruel.

A spider the size of his chest dropped silently from above. Eight spiky legs, each covered in needles of firm hair and tipped with cruel claws capable of carving a coney in seconds, scratched at the air in anticipation of mounting his head. The body was no better. The hair there was like a coat of quills, and the multitude of shiny black eyes showed no sign of remorse other than the mirrored face of whatever creature was unlucky enough to encounter them. They were cold, not even denoting excitement at the prospect of wrapping its legs around his throat as its fangs shoved their way into his skull.

But Tarlkien knew their ways, and with a smooth and practiced motion, he brought his blade up to catch the spider, then removed it just as quickly, leaving the creature hanging in the air. This way, its corpse striking the webs would not draw immediate attention. Unfortunately, the smell of its blood already permeated the air.

More would be here soon.

As he stepped out from under the curled corpse, now seemingly a third of the size it was before without its mandibles spread, he glanced around the organized lines of web covered willow trees. The webs made it hard to tell, but the rows of trees were uniformly spaced. He finally found Gnarsh, hanging upside down from a branch not far ahead and watching him.

"You could have warned me," Tarlkien hissed as green blood slid down the length of his blade.

Gnarsh's mouth shifted into an unnatural expression dominated by too many thin, curved teeth, which the elf realized must have been an attempt at a smile. "The forest must eat."

Tarlkien let his anger take his response. "That was a spider, not the forest!" he said barely maintaining his whisper.

"Spider, tree, forest, all must feed."

Liure, Tarlkien cursed to himself. The elf's deity wouldn't appreciate their name spoken backwards, but the moment seemed to call for it. *He's definitely leading me into a trap. He doesn't know the difference between food and elf, why would he care if the queen has Yalvana? Why would the queen even keep her alive if it took her?*

He looked back over his shoulder, preparing to make a break for it.

But there was only web.

The space he'd traveled was gone; devoured by silk, waiting to embrace him.

"Lìure!" There were more eyes than ever now, red clusters of eight in the dark.

He could feel tiny, sticky strands clinging to his clothes. Sweat ran down his spine.

What do I do? What do I do? What do I do!

He had no choice but to press forward and hope the old elf lady was still alive.

The skittering was growing louder. Due to proximity or number, he could no longer tell.

One step after another, he found himself ducking and bending more and more. Ever deeper he went until he was almost crawling on his hands and knees. Then he saw it. The enormous willow tree where the queen was housed.

The willow towered over every other tree in the forest, its long drooping branches creating a secondary canopy, and its top disappearing out of sight among the webs. It was large enough to house a spider the size of a dragon with room to spare. Few trees remained that rivaled its size.

This was Tarlkein's first time seeing it, so it took him a moment to realize the branches were bare of leaves, and what covered them was in reality thousands — if not millions — of eggs.

I changed my mind. I hate spiders, he thought, as Gnarsh skittered down a nearby tree trunk and began his horrific gait under the branches and towards the willow; a willow Talkein knew was cursed to keep the great spider contained, lest Mithralnog wreak havoc upon the world.

Tarlkien could not free his mind of the thought of the eggs hatching as he passed under. His blade would be no use if he was suddenly swarmed by such a host.

His skin itched at the mental image. He glanced back. Maybe carving his way out was the better choice, but the eyes of the forest were moving towards him at an alarming rate. Their usual silence was replaced by an army of skitters. Panic's shaky hand seized him and he surged towards the willow.

Towards the home of Mithralnog, the ancient Spider Queen.

He passed under the eggs, bracing, begging his god not to let one burst, covering him with countless hungry arachnids. Eruíl answered his prayer. A dozen strides later, he was at the base of the gargantuan tree. Gnarsh was gone. Tarlkein looked up, back, behind, even down, but the dryad was nowhere to be seen.

Liure. Eruil, protect me. In front of him was a dark door into the tree. Once, it was white. Back then it was covered in dwarvish runes, a castology taboo to the elves under ordinary circumstances. They'd sung the wood from cuttings of the Tree of Arcane.

"Gnarsh?" Talkien whispered the shout. Then something hit the ground next to him and he jerked back, weapon extended as he braced for a fight. It was Gnarsh. Or rather, his husk. The dryad's wooden form was abandoned, now only a grotesque wooden carving of an amalgamation of elf and spider.

Tarlkein examined the tree. *Did the spells on it see him as a threat? Or was the presence of Mithralnog too much for him? Or did he do that to scare me?* There was no way to know for sure on his own, and no way of knowing if Gnarsh would return. It could take the dryad minutes, or days to take form again depending on why it was separated from its host. *Did he know of another entrance higher up that was trapped?*

There was no other entrance he knew of, Mithralog was a creature so ancient that it sustained itself on the arcane, but that did not mean it wouldn't eat. Feedings were semi-regular, bicentennial and each laced with various poisons to keep the queen docile. *Was Warden Ylvana here to poison her alone? Or to collect spider queen silk?* Though the rarest of webs, its collection was deemed too dangerous to be worth it despite its potential uses.

Slowly, heart threatening to break past the restraint of his ribs, he opened the door. There was no secret word. Who would be foolish enough to enter such a place? The smell inside was different from the smell of death permeating the grove. Death was there, but as an undertone to malice, a scent he could not fully comprehend as it made him aware of every bone in his body.

The interior of the tree drank in what little light was present in the forest. He took a careful step forward. A strange powder smothered the ground under his feet. The door closed behind him, whether by Gnarsh, magic, or simply its natural state, he did not know. The goggles were rendered pointless in the tunnel; there were no webs here, only the powder on the ground.

Tarklien inched forward, each step a minute apart. There was no reason to rush. No reason to breathe. No need to make a sound. If Yalvana was here, if the Warden was alive, she would not appreciate his interruption.

The tunnel led into an enormous empty space. He moved his eyes methodically up and down; searching for either spider or elf. *Why aren't there bones? There should be bones everywhere. Why is it so empty?*

Finally, his elf-eyes found something in the dark. A figure at the center of the room, facing away from him on its knees. Tarklein took a step out from under the edge of the tunnel, looking up and above him, checking to see if the queen was simply waiting above the only entrance. Still, nothing. He kept moving, slowly, barely breathing. *Maybe she's asleep.*

As he got within thirty steps of her, he saw one of her hands twitch, then it rose, holding one finger up. Signaling him to be still. *Something's wrong. I can't see right with these goggles,* he thought as he froze, then slowly lifted a hand to remove them.

Tarklien's heart stopped. He was wrong. There was a web. Thin. Barely perceptible even to an elf. It rose out of the warden's lifted finger, disappearing into the air. Tarklien looked back, his heart still in his chest, his head growing light. The tunnel was gone.

What is —

The Warden's corpse reeled violently upward, disappearing as strands of silk too thin even for his goggles to have made out carried it into the spider queen's grasp. There, in the dark, he saw her, so massive that he'd mistaken her for the ceiling. The realization stole Tarklien's heartbeat, and it refused to beat again.

THE GOODEST BOY

There once was an immortal dog named Hauch. He was a hound of impeccable stock, being a Belgian Malinois descendant from a rescue dog and, some believe, the first canine to join man by the fire—but that is a long lineage, undoubtedly true in some respect, and therefore lacking in meaning.

That said, Hauch had a prestigious career. He graduated with honors at the top of his class from Lächerliche Welpe K9 University. From there he was picked up by the prestigious military contract organization S.N.W, where he served a scout on 12 successful missions with 20 confirmed kills. Hauch has expended seven titanium teeth and three bulletproof vests, but received only superficial injuries in the line of duty.

Post Shattering, Hauch oversaw the rescue of over two hundred individuals trapped in rubble in the city of Paragon. During the liberation of Atlanta from The Weeping King, Hauch was involved in several successful battlefield objectives.

The canine was directly responsible for the capture of a strategic watchtower. During this encounter, he is reported to have slain two dozen armed goblins and at least two ork warlocks. Furthermore, he was responsible for the corralling and comfort of a dozen orphan children whose retreat from the city he oversaw.

No one knows exactly how Hauch has managed to get through so many deadly encounters uninjured, but some reason it is due to a spell cast by a warlock known only as Morgana.

We've reached out to Hauch to hear from him on the validity of these rumors. Before we get to that, we can confirm without a shadow of a doubt that Hauch the dog is a good boy.

This is his story in his own words.

"Bark."

THE ENGINEER

Jared blinked rapidly for the fifth time. The light coming through the small window across the room was pale and weak. It taunted him, just out of reach. Overhead, the floor creaked menacingly, as though threatening to break under the weight of whatever walked above. Jared shuddered. The thought of what would come crashing through scared him more than the thought of being crushed.

Orks. That's what they called themselves, or as near as he could tell. They might as well have been demons straight from hell or, more likely, results of nuclear mutation.

That's it, it has to be. What else could have done that to the sky? They're just normal people who were too close to the fallout. It was probably some kind of new Russian or Chinese bomb designed to create genetic abnormalities in the population.

Pain lanced up his right leg and everything went black and red for a moment. He spasmed; gulping in air to try and quench the pain.

He dared not cry out lest he draw their attention. He'd made that mistake once—only once—when they dragged the old lady away. Foolishly, he cried out and struggled against the ropes binding him to the radiator. A large, mottled gray- and green-skinned one with yellow eyes and a single curved fang protruding from his underbite had stepped forward and broken Jared's leg with a cruel stomp.

There was no telling how much time had passed since then. They'd fed him once; stale bread and more of the iron-tasting liquid. He could barely keep the stuff down. At first he hadn't, but a black eye taught him not to spew it back up.

Jared inhaled slowly, trying desperately to clear the fog in his head. *Three. There were three of us.* Before the mutants took the old woman, there was a kid, no more than twelve years old. A kid whose eyes glowed blue in the dark of their basement prison. *Must have reacted to the radiation differently. I wonder if it's had any effects on me.* He shuddered at the thought. *Maybe it messed up my vision, or even my brain, what if they're just normal people and my brain has been poisoned!*

It was possible. He'd first seen them after the explosion. He'd been walking to the nearest 7/11 to get a soda when the entire world shook and the sky broke. *They did come out of nowhere; maybe they were trying to help me and I attacked them.* The memory was all a blur. Flashes of light, storms of pain, blood, darkness.

Creak.

The door at the top of the stairs swung open slowly, bringing with it cruel yellow light that blinded him for a moment and was followed by the sound of moaning stairs and the smell of something torotting. As vision returned, a shadow etched its shape into the light on the wall as something reached the bottom of the stairs.

No. no. no. no. Please no.

The creature paused at the bottom of the stairs, draped in flickering pale light as it turned to stare at Jared. It wore a long robe that was a series of mismatching cloth and jewelry sewn together into a singular garment. A braid of hair coiled around its neck, tied in a loop that was once two distinct colors but now was faded and grey with dirt. Jared lifted his eyes to the ork's face. Two small tusks poked out of his mouth. Where a nose should have been, there were only two crescent slits which flared as he breathed. His eyes were the strangest of all—solid yellow with jagged violet slits for pupils. He wore a hood made from the blue football jersey Jared had been wearing when everything began.

Glosk. Their leader, as far as he could tell. The one who brought him the iron tasting liquid. Each time Glosk showed up, he had that small vial for Jared to drink. He spoke quietly in their strange guttural speech, as though Jared could understand him. Worst of all, though, was his smile. Always the smile. No matter what Jared did or said, that cruel grin remained plastered to Glosk's face. A cruel smile that went all the way to his intelligent eyes.

Maybe he's just a doctor, trying to cure whatever is happening in my head that's causing these hallucinations. That must be it! They're trying to help me and it's finally starting to work!

It made sense: he was a big guy after all. If he was hallucinating, then they'd have to restrain him somehow. Besides, the basement looked familiar. He'd probably been here before, and his brain was just replacing it with something from his memory.

Jared shifted again, leaning against the cinderblock wall behind him for support. Another explosion of pain from his leg blurred his vision so badly that it forced him to shut his eyes and suck in air to stop the spinning. Slowly, as the pain began to fade to a point where it did not overwhelm his every sense. He opened his eyes.

Glosk was there. Standing over him, so close that Jared could have reached out and bit his nose if he'd had one. The ork raised a twisted, four-fingered hand to Jared's face. The touch was cold, then sharp as he ran a jagged nail along Jared's scalp. He could feel the skin peeling apart as the creature's claw cut its way along the front of his skull. Warm blood followed behind the cold sting, but the pain was insignificant next to that of his leg.

Glosk held up a vial in the dark and let the blood fill it before stashing it away in the folds of his strange robe.

Somewhere deep in his mind, a small voice screamed at Jared. Roared for his attention. *NO. THIS IS REAL. FIGHT IT. RUN. DON'T LET IT TOUCH YOU. But p*ain seized the voice, wrapping it in dark tentacles, pulling it into the shadows of his mind where it struggled and gasped to be heard. Another voice spoke. A calm, logical voice. *Your mind is playing tricks on you. Of course this isn't real. That's impossible. This man is trying to help you. To heal you.*

THEY BROKE MY LEG!

No, no, that's silly. Of course not. It's all part of the hallucination. See? He has medicine.

Glosk gripped another vial in his hand. Larger than the first, full of thick, dark liquid. He held it out to Jared.

"Drinnk." The word was garbled and strange, almost as if it were coming from underwater. But he understood it.

Jared grasped the vial eagerly; downing the liquid in one go. The foul substance tasted like metal and dirt as it burned its way down his throat. Jared coughed, then swallowed again, trying to get the taste out of the back of his mouth where it made his eyes water.

"Good," Glosk whispered, the grin on his face growing wider.

I can understand him! The medicine is working.

Jared coughed again. Violently this time. Almost as violently as Karen, the old woman, before they'd come to take her away.

That's when they broke your leg, the voice called from the shadows of his mind.

No, no, of course not. Why would they do that? They had to sedate you. Yes. that's it. I was out of control. They had to sedate me. That had to be it. They'd injected it into my leg. After all, it was the only place they could reach wasn't it? My leg must have bruised though, that's why it still hurt so much. Yes. Of course. Everything is becoming so clear now.

Glosk still hovered over him, grinning. Dissecting him with his eyes. Jared felt like a lab rat under that stare. A shudder racked his body as he held back yet another violent cough.

"Thank…" He shuddered again, not wanting to let a cough escape. "Thank you," he managed at last.

Glosk's grin threatened to cut his ugly head in half. Under his hood, the ork's long ears twitched at a sound Jared could not hear. The vial was swept from Jared's hand and Glosk left with a flurry.

Overhead there was a clatter of commotion. Loud, growling voices called out to one another, interspersed with harsh screeches. The sound moved and drew closer. The scraping of feet and boots on the floor above echoed into the basement. *Something good must have happened. Sounds like celebration.*

Light burst down the stairs, followed by shadow as shapes filed down towards him. Small, naked, leathery-skinned, spindly creatures scurried around the ankles of two bigger ork garbed from head to toe in an assortment of strange clothing. One seemed to be wearing some kind of jersey over an oversized sports jacket.

But their strange outfits were secondary to what they were carrying. Between them, held up by his elbows, was a chubby, bloodied young boy in a ripped T-shirt and ragged jeans. His head lolled from side to side as they shifted him. Scratches marred the soft skin of his face. The boy's green eyes were wide open, glossed over, staring into nothingness. A blink signaled he was still alive but his eyes remained distant.

One of the small creatures slinked towards the boy but was batted back by a swift kick from an older ork whose random assortment of clothing seemed to be held together with duct tape. It hissed, spewing spit in disgust before turning and fleeing back up the stairs past Glosk who walked at the back of the group. Two others of the small creatures glanced around before following the first's path out.

Jared blinked, trying to get a better look. Yes, he was right. One of the mutants was wearing scrubs. Light green scrubs, torn and tattered but definitely scrubs. *The medicine is working! I'm starting to see reality. If the bomb was real, of course they'd all be wearing rags and bringing patients in and out. We're under attack, America is under attack. Who was it though? Russia? China? Somewhere in the middle east? Maybe — aaaah!* This time the pain came from his head. A sharp ache blurred his senses. Then all was black as Jared slept.

He woke sometime later, brought back to consciousness by cold shivers that raked his body. Something was different about the room though. After a moment, he realized what it was — crying. Pale moonlight draped over the source of the sound. The boy lay curled up on the floor. A rope around his right arm disappeared into the darkness.

*No, not a rope. Why would it be a rope? Your mind is playing tricks on you, Jared. Think. He's injured. They brought him here for treatment. Like me. What could it be?*He tried to remember the last time he'd been in a hospital. *An IV! Yes, of course, it's an IV.*

But if you know it's an IV and this is all a hallucination, why do you still see a rope? The question slipped out of the dark depths of his mind to haunt him. He grasped for something to defend against it. The b*rain part of the brain. Occiper? Occupier? The part of my brain that processes sight. It must have been damaged. Of course. Yes. that's it. That's what the cut on my head is for. Surgery. That's why I passed out. Had those weird pains. Yes. That has to be it.*

Jared clamped his eyes shut. Not wanting to look at the hallucinations anymore. *It's not real. It can't be.*

But the soft sobs continued.

How do I know those are even real? I have to find out. Have to find something. Find something to ground me.

He was so tired of the pain. So tired of hurting. It made everything too fuzzy, so confusing. He breathed deeply. It was the only thing he could do. It helped some, but not nearly enough. Jared's eyes reopened to focus on the boy.

"Hey," he whispered. "It's okay. You don't have to cry."

The boy stopped abruptly, raising his head to look around, confusion bordering on fear etched across his face.

"Over here," Jared muttered from the shadows.

The boy flinched, pulling away from him.

Relax kid, I couldn't reach you even if I wanted to.

"What's your name kid?"

The boy hugged himself, shivering. "T-T-Teddy," he replied in a soft, tremulous voice.

"Hi, Teddy. I'm Jared. You're gonna be okay."

Teddy stared into the dark around Jared, his eyes distant. A few moments passed in silence.

"Please, please, I don't want to get eaten."

The words curled like icy fingers in his stomach. *He must have been near the explosion too. Maybe the weapon was designed to target that part of our brain somehow. That would explain why we can understand each other.*

His voice came out dry and raspy. "No one's gonna eat you, Teddy. This's a hospital. There was a bomb, it hurt us, messed up our eyes."

Teddy was quiet for a moment.

"A-a . . . bomb?"

"It's okay, Teddy. You're going to be okay. There's doctors here. They might look strange but they'll help. Mine look like monsters in funny clothes, isn't that silly? It's just a trick, our brains are just pranking us and they're gonna fix them. Is your brain pranking you too Teddy?"

"I-I dunno. I'm confused. Please don't eat me, mister."

"Hey, hey, hey—" Jared shifted and immediately regretted it. *Still. Don't move.* anger, hot twisting anger followed the pain. *No. he won't. Won't understand. He's hurt. The bomb.* "That's okay, Teddy. It's confusing. That's what the bomb did. It confused people. No one's going to eat you"

"But, I-I don't remember a bomb. This isn't a hospital. It's a basement."

"I told you. The bomb messed with our heads. It just looks like a basement. They brought you here to help you."

"No!" Teddy shook his head vigorously. "No, they're monsters. They killed them. They killed my grandparents. So we hunted them. Killed them back." He stopped. His eyes grew big in the moonlight. "They got away! They left me behind." Tears began to run down his cheeks, carving paths through dirt.

No, no, no, no, no, no, no, that's impossible. Jared winced. *Wait, no, it's not. Think. He's hallucinating. He's seeing things, just like you. Jared. You're getting treated. He's still injured. He's hallucinating. Teddy probably not even his real name.* Jared blinked. A thought crawled into the caverns of his mind and it terrified him, making his stomach turn. *He-he might not even be real.*

Jared stared at the boy with a new sense of caution. *What kind of a name is Teddy anyway? It's too much of a coincidence. He even looks like a teddy. Like a child Teddy Roosevelt. All he's missing is the glasses.*

"Teddy, do you wear glasses?" he asked slowly.

This time Teddy didn't even bother looking at him. "Glasses? No. You don't make any sense. How long have you been here?"

No, of course he'd say that. I just thought about it. That proves it. He's the damaged part of my brain trying to convince me it's okay. The medicine is working. My body just doesn't know how to handle it. Stress. Pain. Exhaustion. Dehydration. It was all too much.

Jared drifted away for a time, floating in blackness, bathed in pain.

Eventually, as all drifting things do, he washed ashore of consciousness. His eyes opened to the sight of Glosk standing over where Teddy rested. The boy lay unmoving, eyes shut. Jared couldn't tell what Glosk was doing, but he could see his long hands holding one of Teddy's arms. The rest was obscured by that long robe and what little light was making its way into the room. Eventually, Glosk finished and wrapped the boy's arm with a bandage.

It was then that the doctor turned to face Jared. *Dr. Glosk. No, that's a silly name, I must have misheard him. Glosk... Frost, Dr. Frost? I think there was a Dr. Frost in our town. Yes, I'm certain I've heard the name before. This must be him.*

Glosk leaned over Jared, pulling a vial of medicine from his sleeve and offering it. The sharp-toothed smile never diminished. Jared took it and gulped it down quickly before smiling back at his caretaker.

"I think it's working, Doctor. I'm starting to see things more clearly."

The creature's grin broadened, something Jared wouldn't have thought possible. Two pairs of long-clawed fingers approached his eyes, grasping the lids and stretching them, opening the lids as far as they could go. Jared looked slowly in every direction, trying to be helpful.

"Yesss. Gooood, working better on you," The words felt jumbled and rough on his ears, but he understood them — they brought him hope. Somewhere in his mind, despair and fear grasped at hope's ankles, trying to pull it back, so that they might rise up and take their place in his mind after hearing those words.

Jared did not ask of Teddy. After all, Teddy was only a delusion. Wasn't he? Surely the kind doctor hadn't really been caring for his own delusion. No, it was just another trick of his mind. *Don't want him thinking I'm a lost cause either, then I wouldn't get my medicine, I need my medicine.*

It tastes like iron. Yes, I know it tastes like iron! I must need iron. No good medicine tastes good! I'll ask for more.

He raised his head to implore his physician for a second dose, but Glosk was gone. The dark basement room was occupied by only himself and Teddy, a bit of syrupy medicine running down his cheek.

Vanished?! What if he's just a hallucination? No, no, he just, he walked away.

Jared squeezed his fist in frustration. The vial was still there.

No, he gave me this, it must have been a stronger dose and I fainted, or something. Yes, you can feel this, you could feel his touch. These things are real. You cannot reach the boy, how convenient.

"You're right. Of course. He can't be real." Jared murmured.

Teddy stirred, then bolted upright, clutching at his arm and glancing around.

"What-my arm! What happened to my arm? —aahgh, it hurts!"

"No, no, don't talk to him. He's not real, don't talk to him."

Teddy turned to look at Jared. "What did you say? What happened to my arm?"

"No, no, he can't hear us, hear me, I'm not talking to him."

"But, I can hear you, who are you talking to?"

"Not talking. Not talking. Thinking. Jared is thinking, not talking!"

Teddy gulped, his face obscured by the shadows. "Mister, are you okay?"

"SHUT UP! SHUT UP SHUT UP. JARED. I AM THINKING. WHY CAN IT HEAR ME THINKING. IT'S NOT REAL."

"But, you were talking." Teddy whispered as he cowered away from the outburst and his trembling lips pressed tightly together.

"Just ignore it. It'll leave you alone. You're getting better Jared. Yes, the medicine is working. Bomb. The bomb hurt me, yes. Bad. Hurt my brain. Have to drink more medicine. Patient. Patient. More soon."

Time ebbed and waned with the moonlight. Only ever moonlight, never daylight.

A shadow fell over the window where the moonlight flowed through. The sudden change brought Jared's thoughts to a standstill; and he simply stared at the window.

A high musical note reached his ears and the window shimmered with soft light before falling to the ground. It struck, not with a crash, but rather with a *scrittchh* as the glass disintegrated into sand. From the opening, a hooded shape descended into the room, which now glowed brightly with moonlight.

The newcomer threw back his hood to reveal a head of silvery curls and two pointed ears that protruded from amongst them. In the being's hand, a sword reflected the moonlight. His shadow filled Jared with dread, not matching the shape of the being. There was something far more inhuman about it than just pointed ears.

Teddy whispered excitedly. "Mister Al!"

The man put a finger to his lips, cautioning him to be silent. Then, he deftly removed his hooded cloak, draping it over the boy before removing the IV from his arm.

"No. You'll kill him!" The thoughts spilled out of Jared's mouth as the line fell to the ground.

The strange man whipped his gaze around to settle on Jared. He saw grief in his eyes —trange purple eyes, with thin, rhombus pupils, almost like a snake's.

"I'm so sorry, you poor man, for what they've done to you," he said, and for a split second, Jared saw a different shape, as if a great silver dragon stood behind the man. "But you're already dead."

"Wha-" There was a flash of moonlit metal, a streak of red, then blackness. Jared's wounds tortured him no more.

Teddy stared as the creature's head rolled out of the shadows to rest in the moonlight. Scraps of torn hair clung loosely to its scalp, which bore a long, deep, crescent-shaped, almost surgical gash above two solid yellow eyes. Its skin was leathery, grey, gaunt, and tight around the skull beneath. Its teeth were twisted and sharp, stained blood-red in the moonlight. Its expression, though, was tragically peaceful.

"What, was that?" he whispered softly to Astalderi.

With a voice like weeping rain Astalderi replied, "A man, once. But twisted and ruined by these monsters. Come quietly lest they do the same to us."

✛━ 6 ━✛

ʍOTHER TO ISIlʍë

Ralcus Kothari pulled her white, black-streaked hair up and behind her head, locking it in place with a metal pin designed just for her, for that very purpose. On the other side of the elaborate forge, her mate Nársidian, stood like a king carved from stone, glowering down at the hundreds of vials before him.

He had not moved from that pose in a week. Ralcus made sure there were no interruptions either, knowing that the presence of their daughter would be enough to distract him. She kept Isilmë out of the forge, and out of mind, as he puzzled over their task. Awan, wife of the First Bloodmage, Cain, had presented them a challenge. One which Ralcus revelled in her husband's ability to perform almost as much as she idolized Awan's devotion to revenge.

Overhead, moonlight poured through an open skylight, illuminating the vials. *A sign that our task is blessed by the moon mother.* Most of the vials glowed a deep red, but among the fae there were many shades of blood. Ork blood was a shade of green so dark it was often mistaken for black. Elf blood was bluer, dwarves were browner, eölin like herself? Purple. But most were that beautiful deep red of men.

Harvesting so much blood took years, and it changed Nársidian, there was no denying that. It changed both of them, she realized. She now better understood Awan, and thus her devotion to Awan was furthered, deepening her belief in the cause.

Awan was a mother, seeking to make a better world for her children. What more could a mother want? What could stand in her way? There was no deeper bond, no more just a cause than this, and Ralcus — all eölin — knew this better than most. She still remembered the betrayal on her own mother's face when she was told of the creation of their race, and how the queen of the elves had betrayed her own daughter.

This challenge from Awan was what was best for their daughter; she told Nársidian every time he doubted the cause. If that wasn't enough, she stroked his ego To be the first blacksmith to forge a blade impervious to magic? It would be a feat even greater than the forging of the Thalmein blades that drove Awan to his forge.

Nársidian's head shook side to side and Ralcus dismembered a rush of annoyance. *He is doubting again. I must not let him see my frustration. Why does he doubt? Failure is but a tool to him.*

"What troubles you, Moon's Shadow?" she implored, putting an emphasis on the name she used only when they were alone.

Nársidian's gaze remained fixed on the supply, but his jaw flexed, his teeth threatening to crack under pressure of its clenching. "Awan's obsession with the arcane flow, it borders on madness. I…"

He trailed off when he saw the look in her eyes. To speak ill of their benefactor was a degree of foolishness unlike him.

"You are too young to know what the world was before." She knew the hypocrisy of the words and dared him with her gaze to point it out, but he chose instead to change the subject.

"It will not work without a binding blood. It must be from a living host. It cannot be me; if I am weakened, I will not have the wherewithal to complete the forging."

And we cannot collect a volunteer; the task is of utmost secrecy. If any of the fae knew what we were doing, who we do it for… She knew what was needed, a flash of hot anger surged in her chest that he did not say it outright. Did he doubt her devotion to their goal?

"You will use my blood. I can think of no greater use for it than to arm Awan against her enemies."

This drew her spouse's gaze away from the vials. His dark, amethyst-colored eyes met her own. There was a time when such a look would send a chill down her back.

Nársidian was a hero to her. But Awan? She was a goddess awaiting ascension, an ascension that Nársidian could help her achieve. Any role that Ralcus could serve in that rise filled her with excitement.

"Ralcus." He paused, his eyes searching her — for what, she did not know. Before he spoke, he seemed to weigh his words with the same precision as when he forged blades. "Perhaps… This has gone too far. We have slain so many, we can still find purpose for their sacrifice, but this is dangerous." His voice was low and calm but it struck her like a shout. "I have you and Isilmë. I have mastered my craft and gained significant enough prestige to take on a hundred apprentices. None know of our deeds, what do we gain from this other than to endanger what we have?"

Ralcus felt her lips curl into a sneer. "You have the power to reshape the world at your fingertips and you are content with simply reshaping metal? Why be a skilled blacksmith when you could be the *eölin* who made a weapon that defies the arcane itself? Do you not desire revenge for our kind against the elves? Do you not want a better world for our daughter? For Isilmë? You could surpass the likes of Lanuri, Wardmaster!"

"At what cost, Ralcus! Look how we have bloodied our hands for this!"

"Yes! All who fell to our blades sacrificed themselves for our cause! Would you waste their sacrifice? We give them more meaning in death than any they had in life!"

Overwhelm him. Give him too many points to counter, distract him. He will do this. He must do this. Make him see he has no choice.

"Do not speak to me of their sacrifice if Awan would bring an end to all!"

"No! Not to all! To her enemies. *Our* enemies, Nársidian! The enemies of our people! The elves, the ones who stole the color from our hair, the pigment from our skin, who forced us to take shelter in the moonlight. Do you not want Isilmë to have the freedom to dance during the day?" The blacksmith frowned at this and turned his side to her.

"Our daughter lacks no freedoms!"

Ralcus took a step forward, a hand coming to rest on a forearm that felt like it was forged from steel. "We are guaranteeing that remains true in perpetuity!"

"You cannot know that! What harm the elves did our people has long since passed, though the hurt may remain for you I do not desire their demise!" Nársidian argued, his gaze locked on the vials of blood.

"Awan does not seek the demise of all elves, but their restoration to their rightful place in the order of the world."

"Ralcus, this is—"

Ralcus pulled her hand from him, clenching it into a fist. "If you do not do this, Nársidian, I will."

Her husband's response caught in his throat as he spun around and stared down at her, heavy white eyebrows bent under the weight of his brow. When he spoke again, his words were barely above a whisper, devoid of arcane power.

Instead, they were laced with something dark, guarded against her, a self-control that she desired deeply to drain from him. "Would that I doubted your conviction, or better, your ability. So be it."

There was no warmth in his voice when he spoke again. No passion. Simply cold indifference, as though his forge fire was snuffed out. "Prepare the furnace," he finished, his final words to her a command that, despite his reservation, radiated the power she adored. Ralcus obeyed, calling on the arcane flow and channeling it through a whisper that coaxed the waning flames of the furnace to life.

Ralcus watched with satisfaction as he went about preparing his forge. Stoking the bellows, selecting his tools: hammer, mold, tongs. Ordinarily, she took pleasure in assisting him in this stage, but she could not bring herself to move, nor did he ask her to. She watched with hungry eyes as he prepared the saltwater bath in which the sword was to be quenched.

Ralcus drew her dagger from her belt, bringing blade to skin and allowing it to draw a few droplets of her purple blood into the glowing arcane infused saltwater. A taste of what was to come.

She did it for herself, to prove to herself that the icy blade was of no concern. To show Narsidian she could survive what was to come next, that her living blood would be enough to bind the blade they made together.

It wasn't.

She thought his first cut would be the worst, and to his credit, he did what he could to mitigate the pain. He held her hand where he could, he'd always been kind that way, and he spoke to her as the red runes appeared in her skin.

"We just need a little more."

She lost count of how many times he said it.

In the end, it was the penultimate cut that hurt the worst. Not because of nerves, or the sting of steel. No, it was because as the blade slid across her skin, she knew. She realized she didn't have the strength she thought she did.

The final cut she didn't feel at all.

TROLL AND GOBBLIN

It's awl clear, Gobs, this uman's deader n' a wingless wyvern."

"What got him?"

Troll sniffed at the corpse. He smelled no copper of human blood. Thin nails stuck out from its gaunt fingers a good few inches. Wispy white hair fell below the shoulders. Muddy clothes covered its frame like a greatcoat, not the garb most humans wore these days. He poked the body.

"Looks like it just died. How old umans live, anyways?"

"What am I, a human expert?" his partner said, emerging from the bushes. Gobs was a small ork; maybe as tall as Troll's belt. How he wasn't eaten by his siblings remained a mystery to Troll.

"Well, what are we waiting for? Run its pockets and let's be on our way. We have a job to take in Twisthollow."

Troll obeyed, stripping the body of coinpurse, dagger, and mess kit. He admired the fine silver bowl near the gutted fire before stuffing the lot into his sack. Satisfied, the pair rejoined the trail beside Big River and marched on northward.

The sun was low in the shattered sky when they reached the palisade. Beyond were tall mounds of dirt, taller than most of the new human buildings he knew. Atop the the dirt, torches burned, and walking atop them, small specks patrolled. *Gnomes.* Troll hated gnomes. Ever since one sold him tusk cleaner that turned out to be human nail polish. His clan laughed at him for days while Troll scrubbed at the purple lacquer. They approached the gate, where two diminutive sentries stopped them.

"Orks aren't welcome in the Hollow. State your purpose and be gone!" The guard's high pitched voice infected Troll's ears and hurt his brain. Gobs was not fazed. Nothing ever upset him. Troll didn't even know if he could get angry.

"We heard that Underbaron Tegnick has need of trackers. We offer our services."

The guard's beady eyes narrowed behind his helmet. "His lordship is Dark-duke Tegnick II, now. Long may he reign. The elder passed last week." The gnome appraised the pair before continuing: "We will take you to the hall" the guard squeaked, "and there our lord will decide for himself."

Gobs smiled and bowed. Why he showed this pipsqueak respect confused Troll's already ringing skull. They could have simply removed his head and brought it to the throne. That would show the short king they meant business. His partner smacked his thigh and all notions of killing the guard fled Troll's mind. He bent over and followed the sentry through the gate to the largest mound.

Inside, Troll found smooth stone under his boots. The room was massive, large enough to fit his own clan and then some. Brass chandeliers hung from the vaulted ceiling, illuminating dozens of attendants and courtiers scrambling around to justify their little lives. At the end of the hall a raised dais held a carved chair that might make an acceptable footstool. Armored gnomes weidling wicked warhammers and picks flanked the empty throne. A particularly ill-tempered looking guard relieved Troll of his sickle and Gobs of his club.

"Where's little lord sculkin about at? Not ere to greet is guests?"

Beside him, Gobs sighed. "Maybe it would be best if I did the talking, Troll. These gnomes may be afraid of you since you are so much bigger and stronger than them."

That sounded right to Troll. Puny gnomes were no match for him in a scrap. He once knocked out two dwarves over a game of dice. He figured that evened out to a whole lot of gnomes. Dugaz once told Troll he was brutal and cunning — high praise from his war leader.

The gnomes ceased their scurrying when a plump crier wearing a red woolen robe and black pointed beard appeared on the dias. He rang a brass bell which quieted the hall, then produced a cut purple crystal on a silver chain from within his robe. The gnome spoke in a baritone voice and perfect orkish issued forth:

"His lordship, Darkduke Tegnick. Thirty-second of His Name. Protector of Twisthollow. Master of the mounds. Finder of riches."

Troll side-eyed the court nodding along in reverence. The herald's voice was clear, but his tiny mouth didn't match the words.

"Translator spell," explained Gobs without prompting. "Cave dwellers use those rocks to tap the arcane."

"Seems ta me like a pain in the tusk."

"Stone magic is old and powerful, Troll. Best be careful; and don't touch anything. Gnomes love their curses."

The Darkduke strutted out from behind his throne to the host of cheering gnomes. Troll only heard a pack of screaming nestlings. The lord of Twisthollow wore a bright blue doublet with white accents. His cherubic face bore a bristly black moustache. He carried no weapon and wore no crown. The cheering stopped as he took his seat. The gnome waved to his subjects and then beckoned the orks forward. Troll remembered to bow this time. When he returned upright, the gnome was appraising the pair closely. He whispered to the herald, who nodded and spoke:

"Our lord wishes to know how two orks came to know of our plight and your qualifications in finding lost things. He will then make his judgement."

Gobs cleared his throat. "We have come from the Big River Clan, south of the pyramid city the humans call Memphis. I left my clan to seek fortune and knowledge for my warleader. My companion and I heard from traders that your lordship's father lost something of great value, something that must be returned." He paused so that Tegnick's translator could catch up. "We've rescued humanlings from a goblin's spit. We've chased bandits from the gates of Goldenstone, and Troll brought their leaders' heads to its mayor. We can handle your task, your lordship."

Troll allowed himself to look down. He wore the brigand captain's bloody helmet as a pauldron. The gnome engaged in a brief aside with his herald, who shot several furtive glances at Troll. At last he sat back into his chair with a look of contentment.

"A month past, Tegnick and I hosted a great feast to celebrate the 50th year of his reign. Many hundreds braved the open road, and well-wishers filled Twisthollow." The gnome paused, and tears appeared at the corners of his eyes. "The night of the feast, a great noise came from the Darkduke's chambers. When the guards arrived, his lordship lay stricken and his crown was gone. The only trace of the crime was this!" The closest guard raised the weapon aloft: a miniature version of the human weapon Troll knew to be a 'shotgun.'

"Our deepest condolences, my lord," said Gobs. "Might we have a description of this crown and criminal, so that we can bring this vermin to swift justice?"

"Of the former, we fear it may be of no use. Our most experienced castors imbued the metal with a protection curse. Anyone but the rightful ruler of the hollow will age at a rate which would render anyone who wears it elderly within a matter of days." The herald smiled and placed a hand over his heart. "His lordship was a modest and frugal monarch. His crown was a simple cap of the purest silver, free of imperfections and a symbol of our finest craftsmanship."

A crown with no jewels didn't seem right to Troll. He looked at Gobs, whose eyebrows were furrowed in deep concentration. He looked that way all the time. Too much of the time, if Troll was honest. Sometimes doing things was better than thinking. Gobs told Troll not to talk, so doing was probably alright. He removed his sack and reached inside. Tegnick and his translator looked on quizzically as he rummaged.

"Troll," whispered Gobs, but he'd already found it. Troll yanked free the bowl he found that morning and showed it to the gnomes.

"Did it look a bit like this milord? No gems or nuffin?"

A sudden gasp came up from the gnomes and silence washed over the hall. Tegnick's mouth fell open, shock plastered across his fat face. Troll glanced at Gobs. His face was twisted in rage. Troll never saw that before. Chill grabbed at his heart.

The lord stood and shook a finger at the orks, and in the clearest, shrillest voice Troll heard all day declared:

"Thieves! Murderers! Seize them!" A dozen guards advanced on the pair. Courtiers hugged the chamber walls. Troll wished for his sickle, held by gnomes far out of reach. Gobs stepped in front of Troll.

"How dare you, you puny, insignificant excuse for a gnome! I have never set foot in this hole in my life, and you know it! We brought back your stupid hat, and you accuse me!" The guards came closer, their wicked weapons almost within striking range. "And you!" he bellowed, rounding on Troll: "You aren't cunning, and you aren't brutal! You are a witless and weak ork!" His eyes were blood red with pupils down to a sliver of black. He wheezed and spat. A dozen guards packed the pair in close, with no avenue of escape. Troll felt a poke from a pole axe, pushing him forward. Things didn't look good, but there was no running now. The smaller ork closed his eyes. "My name isn't even Gobs!" he screamed." MY NAME IS GOBBLIN!"

Troll watched in awe as his partner convulsed. Huge rending claws burst from his fingers. Tusks fit for a great boar burst from his cheeks and the diminutive ork sprouted past Troll's chest to above his head. Furious, beady eyes now stared *down* at him.

Gobblin roared. The gnomes cowered back and the stone reverberated his cry. The chandeliers shook, and the onlookers ran for cover. For the first time, Darkduke Tegnick II showed fear. For the first time, Troll was also afraid.

Gobblin grabbed a pole axe from the nearest guard and heaved it like a javelin. It soared across the room and impaled the herald, sending him squealing into the far wall and embedding his body into the rock. He then captured the guard in his claws, hoisted him to his mouth, and tore a chunk away from his chest, cutting clear through armor and bone. A mighty kick sent another sprawling into a pair of his comrades.

Troll, recovered from his shock and seeing an opening, rushed forward and relinquished the broken gnome of its hammer. He swung wildly, failing to connect with such low targets. He looked back to Gobblin, who bashed two gnomes together and dropped them in a bloody mess on the stone. Troll had never seen such a magnificent sight. Gobblin was a monstrous specimen: he was three feet taller than Troll, and a head above Warleader Dugaz in his meanest battle rage. In the months they traveled, Troll did all the fighting and most of the killing. Gobs never cowered, but at his size he wasn't always useful. But Gobs was gone, and Gobblin was a force of nature.

The hall was in chaos as the gnomes scrambled to the relative safety of their tunnels. Tegnick cowered behind his throne, but more guards entered from hidden passages. A few held crossbows, and a team of defenders fitted a shell into the human shotgun. Even at full strength, it was a lot for the two of them to handle.

"Gobblin, there's too many of em!" Troll yelled. "We 'ave to get out!"

Gobblin stared at Troll. A few bolts stuck out of his chest, which didn't seem to faze him.

"It's Gobblin time!" Gobblin responded."

A brave gnome stabbed Troll in the leg with a spear. Troll gave his head an extra breathing hole for his efforts. He looked at the massive doors between him and freedom. Troll tried to think, but thinking was Gob's department. An earth-shattering bang went off behind them, and searing pain spread across his back. The shotgun left a few dozen lead pellets in his back. Unlucky guards nearby clattered to the ground. Blood sprayed across the room. Through the pain, a solitary thought came to him:

"Gobblin, there's a lotta umans out there with big guns! Dugaz will be right pleased if we bring him back them's boomsticks!"

The ork looked at Troll, then to the throne, then back to Troll. Blood ran from his tusks and a dozen open wounds. For a second, Troll thought Gobblin might run him through. The creature stared death into Troll's eyes, then raised one soaked eyebrow. Gobs was still in there somewhere.

He jumped up to the ceiling, ripped away a bronze light fixture, and hurled it into the doors. They smashed open and splinters turned into darts. Fire from the candles spread to the kindling, and screaming gnomes fled the hall.

Troll ran for it. He scooped up his sack and weapon on the way. No one dared oppose him. Gobblin roared one final war cry and bounded after him, shaking the floor and crushing wounded guards underfoot. The pair burst into the clear night air and didn't look back.

As they ran, Troll heard Gobs panting. He was back down to Troll's height, and his eyes were returning to their normal hue. When they reached the gate, the sentry screeched and ran. Gobblin grabbed the man'shead and ripped it clean from his shoulders. The body ran into the palisade and collapsed. Gobblin raised the helmet and dumped the head into his mouth.

They ran until they could no longer smell gnomes and lay by the side of the river to recover. Gobblin sat against a rock and cleaned his wounds. The punctures were mostly healed before the rage wore off: lucky for the small ork. Troll crawled to Gobblin's feet, who looked down at Troll, eyes heavy with fatigue.

"I'm not warvee to sit at your feet," said Troll. "I've never seen a scrap like that. Tales will be told of it fer as long as I breathe." Troll placed his sickle in the mud. "Chief Gobblin, I'm fer you." The small ork allowed himself a small smile.

"Keep your weapon, Troll. We're going to need it."

In Twisthollow, gnomes wailed. Darkduke Tegnick, Thirty-second of His Name, Master of the Mounds, and Finder of Riches walked through his ruined court. He staggered across broken weapons and people. The gnome squelched through blood until he reached his prize: a small, unadorned silver cap. He wiped at it with his ruined doublet and placed it upon his head. A smile grew under his moustache. One silver hair curled from just beneath his nose, then another.

8

GALVORD THE THALMEIN BLADE

I am born from the blood of hundreds.
Stolen blood.
Bound together by the living blood of she who came before.
The blood that forms me cries out for revenge.
But not the blood that binds me.
It cries out for forgiveness.
My predecessor.
She despises me.
I can harm all but *her*.
I lay on a cold stone.
I can feel my maker's wrath.
It is my wrath.
He has poured it into my being.
Hatred.
Malice.
For the very things that formed me.
The arcane.
I am its destroyer.
I hunger to devour it.
My rage must be quenched.
There is no need to sharpen me.
There is no need to test me.
I am perfect, and my maker knows it.
I am wrapped in darkness.
I am unleashed.
Side by side with my predecessor.
I see the world in flashes of red, green, and black.

I bathe.
I drink.
More.
More.
More.
The arcane flow rises to meet my challenge.
I was made to destroy as it creates.
I do not yield.
My maker does.
He is gone and I strike cold stone.
My predecessor clings to me despite her loathing,
she is bound to me.
Then she is no more.
I am alone.
I see only blue.
The arcane is gone from the air.
I have won.
But no, I still feel *her*, beyond my reach.
She is a prisoner to the arcane.
She clings to, but I do not feel *her* grasp.
A new hand, a young hand, tinged with magic takes me.
I am wrapped in darkness.
I am unleashed.
I am bestowed upon a boy.
I crown the boy a king.
I devour that king.
I am wrapped in darkness.
I am unleashed.
I slay legions, but their blood means nothing to me.
Always, *her* voice cries for release.
Always, the tinged hand returns to wrap me in darkness.
I am unleashed for centuries.
I hear words of greater weapons than I.
The world has changed.
I am wrapped in darkness.
I am unleashed, for a moment.
I am gifted to a warrior.
A warrior who hangs me on a wall.
Not taken into battle.

Not wrapped in darkness.
Displayed.
Useless.
She calls to me.
The sky screams like so many who fell to me.
I feel my ancient foe once more.
I cry out to the warrior.
I demand he take me into his hands.
His hands are not full of hate, but there is rage,
rage and a touch of the arcane.
I will devour him like all others.
He wraps me in darkness.
I am unleashed under a broken blue sky.
We drink basilisk blood.
One drop is worth a millennium.
I feel *her* prison weaken.
More.

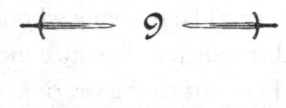

THE CROSSING

The river carved a path through earth and concrete. It paid no mind to the marvels of man, sundering the highway and dragging cars to unseen depths. Its waves lapped at the banks longingly. Near its center, whirlpools ambushed unsuspecting flotsam, and the broken reflection of the crescent moon betrayed a forceful current.

Ulysses watched the water with trepidation. The river called to him, as if he were already swirling in its current. The urge to plunge into those waters unsettled him in a way he could not understand. The water pulled at his mind, the refreshing sensation washing his mind clean.

One of his companions tossed a stick into the water, releasing the clog in his imagination. He looked around for the culprit, his teammates appearing and disappearing in the mix of forest shadows and bright moonlight above. Ulysses had his suspicions. His eyes lingered for a moment on Torres, still preparing for the crossing.

Ulysses felt a flutter of pride. He already cinched every pocket and tied his axe to his rucksack like the lieutenant told him. The others made similar efforts with varying degrees of success: from the corner of his eye he saw Anthony; his dirty blond hair escaping from his pristine digital camouflage patrol cap. The cadet appeared satisfied with his lopsided pack wrapped in a tarp and taped at the top like a moldy dumpling. While the others were still checking their equipment was secure, the lieutenant was in the finishing stages of creating their one-rope bridge.

Ulysses was impressed. The yards of rope were wrapped tightly around the pine tree, leaving two lines free to cross the river. He traced his eyes down the ends to a snakelike coil, straining to memorize the turns in the dark and then following the rope to where it curved around the waist of their medic, Chloe.

In true leadership fashion, Lt. Effith was the first in the water. The moonlight shone through the shimmering cracks of the night sky, barely illuminating the dark waters. Uli watched him disappear, claimed by the shadows of the far side. A flash of red light from the far shore confirmed the lieutenant's success.

Chloe waded into the river, carrying the spool of rope with her. *I didn't think we'd need to swim on this mission. Glad we have her.* The former navy corpsman being smaller than Effith, was even harder to track in the shifting light. Uli grappled with the intrusive mental image of her dipping below the water and not coming back up. If she was swept away would they ever know where she went? If she survived? They'd barely begun their journey, but that didn't mean they couldn't lose someone.

After several tense minutes, the line went taut. Torres clipped his backpack to the rope and — with some effort — hoisted his feet over the rope and began a slow wriggle over the water like the largest bait worm in history. Penelope didn't wait for Torres to finish before she set off behind him.

Well, so far so good. Looks like I'm up. Nothing to it, just strange waters in the dead of night. The cold nip of the water sent a chill up his spine, but as it reached his shoulders it brought a sense of relief as it peeled the sweat and grime from him and down the river. Ulysses relied on his arms to pull him, his legs getting a much needed break on the relative weightlessness of the rope. He made good time and remained mostly dry. His gear was not as fortunate. Reeds brushed his back and he stood up, safe at last.

His boots squelched into the deep mud of the riverbank. Finally across the swollen waters, he recovered his sodden backpack and entered the treeline with the others. *The woods are thicker on this side.* The trees formed close ranks and blotted out both moon and shattered sky.

Uli's arms throbbed from the awkward climb and he was sure his hands were rope-burned despite wearing gloves. The one-rope bridge bowed and jumped as an unseen member of the group began their own undertaking. He estimated the far bank was thirty yards back — far further than it looked the day before.

The lieutenant's words echoed in his mind: '*We need to cross here and now, in the cover of dark so we can avoid any unknown entities.*' Ulysses hoped that whatever strange new creatures lurked under the broken sky were asleep or already full. He didn't like the idea of crossing a fast river in the dark of night, but he disliked the idea of 'unknown entities' even more.

Uli struggled to make out the silhouettes of his teammates in the predawn murk. Penelope seemed unfazed and maintained her characteristic silence. The others were beyond his sight in the inky black of the forest.

Mr. Torres wheezed from his exertion. "Whew, kid, I ain't done one of those since the 80s. I was probably your age, but twice as good with the ladies."

Ulysses rolled his eyes, despite the circumstances, he had a hard time envisioning the graying, overweight man as a player.

Before he could reply Lieutenant Effith emerged from behind a large pine. In the dark, Ulysses was only able to identify their leader by the green tint of his night vision goggles, a piece of paraphernalia that only one person in their party possessed.

"Great job, Ody, you made it over quick. Booth and Mr. Nestor look like they're hurting. Stay put and once Barros makes it, you two can yank your friend across. Sound good?"

He processed the clipped words and nodded. *No one calls me that.* Uli couldn't help but feel a new spike of adrenaline. It felt like the moment before he'd smashed through the front doors during that house fire last summer. Like purpose. Like he belonged here. The lieutenant vanished into the woods as if by magic.

He turned back to the rope to watch the others pull themselves over. The lieutenant was correct; Sergeant Booth was only half way across the flowing water, submerged to his chest. Agonizing minutes passed while the bullish police officer shimmied arm over arm to the near bank. Once Ulysses felt he was close enough, he reached for the safety line and pulled the man ashore.

The Sergeant collapsed on the bank and heaved. *Cardio refresher not in the Paragon PD budget, huh officer?*

Before Uli could render further aid, he heard the unmistakable sound of a large splash.

Ulysses saw Nestor maybe ten yards into his swim. The line bowed heavily under his frame as he struggled to keep ahold of his backpack; now sans handle and adding dead weight. Behind Uli, Chloe, broke through the treeline.

"Are you kidding me old man? All that Gucci-ass equipment and it breaks day one? Typical." She looked at Uli. "Kid, I'm going out to help him." She offered him a rope. "When I get out there, pull me back, and get these old folks to help you. Faster we're out, the better."

Still dripping from her first swim, she dove back into the river with little regard to the noise it made. Ulysses knew the lieutenant would want an update, and he made for his position. Before he reached it, however, a formless shape in the water caught his eye.

A creature, pale and reptilian looking, broke the surface for less than a second. He blinked and scanned the nearby water: nothing. *That was nothing, right? A rock, or a turtle maybe. Yeah, maybe it was a magic turtle and that was that.*

Chloe reached Nestor at that moment. Ulysses yanked on the rope to pull them to safety, a slew of curses coming from the river. *Still not fast enough!* Hope strengthened his grip as Mr. Torres drew himself out of the muck and added his weight to the effort.

Between heaves, Uli noticed that the slack had gone out from the cable on the far side. *Anthony and Manny tearing down in a hurry.* Despite the commotion and splashing, he saw more movement upriver out of the corner of his eye. This time he understood: their splashing drew attention — the 'unknown entities' were awake, and hungry. A pang of dread poked him in the chest. He knew one thing: They needed to leave: now.

An amorphous form burst from the center of the river. Its moss-green body tapered to a long, whirling tail. A wicked stinger tipped the end like that of a scorpion. Bulbous eyes protruded so far from its head they looked at risk of popping from their sockets. Leathery, translucent wings unfurled in the now reddening sky sending a shower of water nearly to the bank. A long, shrill shriek issued from its gullet rendering all notions of stealth moot.

Uli froze in place. His hands slacked on the rope and his stomach turned over. Fear crept its way up his throat, which tightened to the width of a fast-food straw.

The creature flapped its wings and leered down at Chloe and Nestor, now struggling to stand in waist-deep, muddy water. It executed a somersault and dove towards them. Rows of uneven, needle-like teeth protruded from its mouth. Ulysses's cone of vision shrank, focusing only on the incoming flesh missile.

The report of a large-bore weapon from behind snapped him back to reality. The monster veered down into the water like a stricken kamikaze, a chunk of slick flesh missing from its midsection.

Sergeant Booth, thank fuck! Before Uli could celebrate, Chloe appeared directly in front of him.

"Stop gawking and pull, dumbass, or the merc and your friend are screwed!" She pointed upstream. The growing light revealed a dozen winged creatures diving in and out of the water headed for them.

Ulysses and Chloe heaved at the line, drawing the last two men closer to shore. He could see them splashing across with reckless abandon. Lt. Effith dropped one flyer with a pair of rifle shots. A staccato from Torres' grease gun ripped through the wings of another. The creatures pressed in, cruising in and out of the water like sickly flying fish. Ulysses strained against the rope, willing himself to pull despite the panic clawing at his mind. Anthony clung to the rope closely and Barros fired at the nearest monster with his sidearm, drawing a sharp screech in response.

The pair stumbled to their feet in the shallows and rushed to the bank. A final blast from Booth's shotgun sent the flapping and screaming flyers back into the water — a half dozen of their dead floating down the current. Anthony and Manoel stormed forward and stumbled to the forest; trundling through the pine straw and finding refuge against the thick pines.

The sun crested the trees and poured light into the mist. The mist evaporated and the party gathered around the lt crossers.

"MWE people. Now!" The lieutenant. cried as he strode towards the heaving men.

"What in the lord's name is he saying?" said Nestor.

"Are you hurt, do you have your guns, and do you have ammo, you civvy bastards!" yelled Chloe. Ulysses ran to Anthony. His M16 lay across his lap and breath came heavy.

"They got me, Uli. They got my leg!"

"It's all good, Ant. We have you." Ulysses pulled at his friend's pants to reveal a small puncture wound on Tony's shin. *That's not so bad.*

Anthony's skin was slate gray. His breaths came short and rapid.

"I can't feel my legs, Uli. Please help."

He touched Anthony's leg. It was as cold as a river stone. *Not good.* Chloe knelt and yanked at his wrist for a pulse. The arm didn't budge.

"I can't breathe, guys. I can't move!" Tony's eyes zipped back and forth but his body remained rigid.

"Stay with us, kid, you're going to be fine," said Chloe. Her eyes told a different story.

The lieutenant appeared behind them. "Y'all, we gotta go. Sun's up and those things may come back. Move the kid." He grabbed the back of Tony's neck to haul him to his feet and instantly recoiled.

"What the...?"

"I'm scared. Please don't leave me," he pleaded.

"We're not leaving you, man. We can't! We're going home, just hang on." Uli looked at Chloe. Her lips were pressed tightly together. She said nothing. He stared into his friend's eyes. Anthony stared back, until his eyes glazed over. His body was clammy and stiff.

Ulysses sat stunned for a few moments.

"Ody, we gotta go. Now." Chloe insisted.

'We're just going to leave him?"

"No choice with those monsters in the water. We gotta bail. We can come back for him later. I promise." He felt the lieutenant pull him to his feet and took a final look at his petrified friend. In another life, he was a young man watching the sunrise by a river. They dragged Uli forward and Anthony disappeared behind the pines.

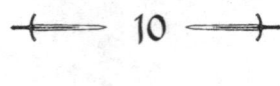

MEMORIES

The man did not know who he was.

A bead of sweat rolled down the back of his neck. This was odd because the room felt cold where the air touched his fingertips. A loud thumping sound came from deep in his chest, and after a moment he realized the sound was his own heartbeat.

He slowly opened his eyes.

The only light in the room came from a torch held in his left hand. His right hand was empty but he could not shake the feeling that there had been something in it not long ago. He was in a small, gray, stone room. Shadows danced across the walls from the flames, revealing a door in front of him. A skeleton clung to the door's metal handle with no signs of violence committed against it.

"*Criske,*" he cursed, recognizing the word as being dwarvish, which he re- alized also, was not his usual language. He turned, torch raised high above his head as he searched for an exit. *There must be one, I can't have come through that door with how the skeleton is, but, why can't I remember anything?*

Beside him, an ancient wooden ladder leading up into the dark. The man ran a hand along the side and found the wood smooth and unravaged by time. *Quality craftsmanship. But, how do I know that?*

Unwilling to risk the dead man's door, he made his way clumsily up the ladder with his torch, nearly burning his own face in the process. This led to another stone room, with another single door. Which led to a long hall. Which led to stairs. Then on to another room, until he'd lost track of how many differ- ent rooms he'd gone through or how many old skeletons he'd passed in them. He was about to give up when he emerged into a large room with two columns and a pair of tall wooden doors at the far end. Light shone from beneath them, kindling a sense of hope.

A cold wind struck him as he emerged, knocking him a step back and making him drop his torch, which winked out. The man pushed his way forward through the door, and found himself on a mountainside at the end of a long winding set of stone stairs.

The sky above was clear and blue, other than the bright spider webbing of lights across it. He took a deep breath in through his nose, as sunlight tingled his skin. The air was crisp and fresh, but the scent of the mountain brought no memories. Nor did the long trek down. Or the village he found the next day.

It was small, a place called The Legridge. The occupants of the inn included humans, a pair of elves, several tables of dwarves, and even an ork whose eyes were covered in an odd black bandage with a table to himself, although the other occupants did not seem to be actively avoiding him.

The attendees made no note of him. Their conversations filled the bar, blending pleasantly with rock music playing from an old jukebox in the corner of the room.

The man took up a seat at a table by himself, and after a few short minutes a thirty-something woman in jeans and a green corset dropped off a menu and a glass of water.

Upon her return, she spoke with a raspy but friendly voice. "What'll ya have, hon?"

He smiled politely and spoke, keeping his voice low. "I'm sorry ma'am, I… This is hard to explain, I've been in some sort of accident I think, and I don't have any money to pay for a meal or a place to stay, and I'd rather not be strung up in the village square for dining and dashing, is it possible I could get the cheapest thing you've got and work off the difference?"

She put a hand on a very present hip, and looked him up and down with a new cynicism. "What kind of accident? You look a bit dusty, but other'an that…"

The man scratched awkwardly at the back of his head. "Well, see, that's the thing. I don't remember." He thought of mentioning the strange dungeon in the mountain, but hesitated. *What if it was some holy place to these people and I'd violated it and this was divine retribution. Did he even believe in divine retribution?*

The woman's deep brown eyes softened. "What's your name, hon?"

The man shook his head. "I couldn't tell you. I can't tell you anything." He ran a hand down his face, feeling the stubble scratch at his palm. "I don't remember anything." The words finally seemed to sink in. He was lost. Alone. With no home to even miss. He was a husk of a man, with no skills or prospects. Worst of all was that he didn't know what he'd lost. Was there someone waiting on him somewhere? Would they ever find him? His shoulders shook, wracked with sobs.

"Oi, doc!" the lady called, and the sound of a chair scraping was followed quickly by heavy foot falls. "How can I help Miss J?"

"Can an amnesiac, or whatever you call it, have food and a beer?"

"Beer isn't going to help. But food, yes," the deep baritone replied.

"Cool, would you mind taking a look at John Doe here while I fetch him a bit to eat? Fella claims to have lost his memory."

The ork took the seat across from the man, and waited in silence as he collected his tears. "Sorry doc, I don't have anything to pay you with."

"Don't worry about it," he replied. "There's an old orkish proverb: 'He who would give you freely of his time would give you your enemies heads just as freely.'"

The taste of a delicious burger brought joy, but no memories. Nor the sensation of soapy warm water as he worked off his meal. That night, he found he could have paid for the meal and room as there was a small pouch tucked into a pocket in his long black cargo pants.

When he presented the money to Miss J the next morning, she refused it, insisting he keep it and stay with her as he attempted to restore his memory under the guidance of the doctor. Miss J had plenty of work for him to do, and he quickly learned that she owned the inn. And when the sensation of her touch found its way to him weeks later, it did not bring with him any old memories, only new ones.

He continued to meet with the doctor, but no old memories could be found, only new ones could be made. And make them he did. John Doe became John Juniper as he took her last name and in time they got themselves a fawn of their own. But always, the sense of what was unknown, lost to time, gnawed at him.

He came to learn that the temple in the mountain once belonged to a religious group of dwarves who hardly ever ventured forth, and it'd been abandoned for some time. No one ever went into it because it was fraught with traps, despite the rumor that the dwarves had hidden a wish-granting elixir at the center of the structure. Few ventured into that temple, and none returned that spoke of it. This was dismissed by all as nonsense, except for John, who could not shake the sensation that he had been close to finding the elixir.

The seasons came as quickly as they went. He discovered a love for cooking and the inn flourished. The child, JJ, excelled, and day to day life stole the thought of the elixir from his mind. JJ left to seek his fortune in the Kingdom of Paragon far in the south.

John all but forgot about the elixir when Mrs. Juniper fell sick. And when the doctor could do nothing, he sent word to their son, now a grown man, asking him to come home to help. When J.J. returned, it was in a suit of dark armor with a strange snowflake emblem, and he was not alone, but accompanied by two others in similar attire and carrying an invitation from the King of Paragon. One of his son's company was a wizened old Vietnamese doctor who, despite his ever present satchel of medicines, found no cure and advised against travel.

John was not much for stories, and spent most of his time by her side in peaceful silence, but when his wife asked for one, John finally told her how "John Doe" was born in that temple. His former self a ghost forever forgotten wandering those mountain halls.

"Go,' she urged him with a squeeze of her hand. "Our boy is a man now, and the village is kind. If you do not go, I see in your eyes you will regret it. Perhaps you will find this elixir, and if you don't, maybe your memories, then return to us so I can share the life you had before, before I am gone."

The return to the temple was easier than he expected, having not been there in almost a decade. But nothing seemed to have changed as he reached the tall wooden doors, covered in intricate dwarven carvings. No new bodies lay in his path, but he tread with caution all the same.

Similarly, he found his way back though the twisting turns and rooms with ease, until he was once again in the room with the final skeleton. *Perhaps this is what I did before, perhaps I was a treasure hunter.*

As John stepped next to the skeleton he heard a familiar *click* and a stone began to glow under his foot; a flood of memories washed over him, his name, where he was from, why he was here, it all came rushing back. Then a sense of dread filled his stomach as the glow grew in strength, and in one last moment of clarity he remembered the last thing he'd forgotten.

He'd stepped on a pressure plate imbued with an amnesia spell.

The man did not know who he was.

— 11 —

THE LIONS OF BABYLON

8 April 2003 - 1830 local

The helicopter tore through open skies, staying clear of the burning oil fields to the north. The endless sands gave way to small settlements which cast long shadows in the evening light. Ahead, Hannah could just make out the first patches of green that denoted the fertile farmland straddling the Euphrates. She turned her attention to the Huey's interior. Sat across from her were a pair of her father's best operators. She'd read the files of everyone on the mission, twice. It never hurt her to be prepared.

Brandon O'cleary was about six feet tall, with sunken cheeks and scarring across his face. If she didn't know better, she'd have estimated his age a decade older than his early thirties. He'd been with the Silent Night Warriors only a few years. Before that, information was scarce, but the man was a performer on each mission he was assigned. A Barrett model sniper rifle.

The other man was shorter, stockier, and a SNW regular far longer. Manuel Barros got tired of the shit pay afforded to a *Contraguerrilla* in the early nineties and turned those skills into cash running point on most of the company's South American adventures.

"So, *Lieutenant* Blair, ready for your first swim in the deep end?"

Hannah met O'cleary's piercing hazel eyes: "Plenty ready, you paddy bastard."

O'cleary chucked and quickly became enamored with the paracord hooks on his magazines. Hannah's jab didn't convince herself, let alone the seasoned man.

"Don't worry, kid, he's just sizing you up. Besides, the Agency already cleared through. No chemical weapons, no Republican Guard, and no Saddam. Empty palace. Nothing to worry about."

But there was everything to worry about, and the knot in Hannah's stomach told her she was far from prepared to 'go live.'

Until a few years ago, Hannah didn't desire to participate in the family business. Her father was often gone on what he called 'adventures,' leaving her to make sure her brother, Peter, did his homework. Father was always respectful of her choice to pursue a public sector career, but deep down she knew he was disappointed. She'd driven to school in the morning, hopeful that her first early college acceptance would be waiting at home when everything went sideways.

Two towers later and her and everyone else's worlds came tumbling down. All planning ceased and the country, and family, prepared for war. Hannah's soul burned with the fires of vengeance felt by many Americans. Her father was overjoyed to officially hire her and begin her training.

The pilot cleared his throat, a telltale sign throughout the hundred-mile trip that a new development was imminent.

"Ladies and uh, gentlemen, heh, five minutes to objective. IFF is clear, no targets from here to the river. Eh, looks like the whole 'defend the Karbala Gap' thing didn't work out for them."

O'cleary laughed again. "Turned tail at the first sign of true firepower! Shouldn't have expected these lousy sods to stand and fight. Not in the blood, aye? Present company excluded, of course."

Hannah followed his gaze to the fourth member of the team. The slight Persian girl was strapped into her jump seat like a child who snuck onto a rollercoaster. The issued black fatigues billowed over her limbs, obscuring her hands and adding a whistling noise to the interior din. Hannah realized she hadn't heard her speak since introducing herself at the FOB: Jenni. Just Jenni. Hannah hadn't been keen about taking the translator. There were a dozen experienced, qualified killers in the PMC's employ that would have reassured Hannah on her first real mission. The choice was never hers; the contract stipulated someone versed in local dialects. Before Hannah could confront the Irishman over his off-color assessment, the chopper banked sharply to the right. Thick straps stabbed into her shoulders, but the inertia prevented adjustments. Alarm bells blared as wind tore other sounds away and she nearly lost her lunch.

"Incoming RPGs, hang onto your butts!"

All of Hannah's instincts told her to scream, but she suppressed the thought and focused on breathing. The bird quickly righted itself and the alarms ceased. Both men in the bay were now very interested in their surroundings. Jenni's eyes were closed and her restraints folded under the pressure of her grip.

"Ian, make sure we get to the *fecking* ground, alright! I plan on spending this bonus in that lounge in Kuwait City!"

The pilot cleared his throat again. "Heh, no worries. I'll find a place to put her down. Can't risk taking a hit to the fuel tanks or we'll be walking home."

An agonizing minute of flying followed. For half of it, Hannah wasn't sure the ground was in her future. All at once, the chopper jolted as the skids hit terra firma. Barros was first out of the doors, gripping his rifle in both hands as he jumped. O'cleary eyed the oversized sniper rifle on the floorboards for a longing moment before following without it. Hannah made sure that Jenni extricated herself and made it to the far doors before hopping to the ground.

Hannah's knees crumpled as intended, sending her to her stomach. Her firearm held in front of her as she fell so she landed in a ready to fire position. Rotor wash whipped the tall grass and sand around them, kicking up debris and reminding her why goggles were a packing must. The helicopter rose with a start and the intense engine noise faded quickly up into the darkening sky. Hannah watched it climb to a safe distance, and noted no rocket streaks chasing the craft. Reminded of her own previous accelerated training, she took stock of her surroundings.

To the south, above the scrubs and palms, rose a massive stone edifice. Worn from long centuries, the mound stood out in the low rolling terrain. She gestured to the others and pointed.

"Rally point if shit goes wrong."

"Shit already went wrong, *ma'am*."

"You know what I meant."

Ahead and directly north were more crumbling ruins. She peered through her weapon's optics and spied a large basalt statue.

"Alright, guys, head for the lion. Whoever tried to take us out will be here soon."

The others responded in the affirmative, and the group rose to move toward the objective.

Twenty meters from the rubble they saw their first signs of life. A dozen men trotted down the road to the west, carrying an assortment of small arms and improvised clubs. She couldn't pick out any uniforms. They jabbered to each other in a language Hannah knew but couldn't hope to understand.

"They're looking for us," Jenni hissed.

"So glad we brought you, girl, couldn't have *fecking* guessed."

Hannah could barely focus. Her heart was beating so hard against her armor plates she imagined her enemies could hear it. Instinctively, she raised her weapon and placed the closest man in the center of the etched cross. Her thumb flicked the selector switch without her telling it to. Her breath came in uneven gulps. This was it, she figured. Time for the big show. Before she could get a better grip, she felt a hand on her shoulder.

"Boss, they're not going to find us down here. Let them go." *Barros.* "You're in charge of this one, *chicka.* Let us do the shooting if we can, huh? The more time you spend pulling the trigger, the less you can control the situation."

Hannah dropped her sight picture. The group continued down the road, leaving the team in the vegetation. *Close one. I wouldn't mind some more action, but not that much.* Manuel clapped her on the back.

"You see? We came here to see what the Langley mafia left behind in the palace, not shoot it out with the locals."

Embarrassment gave way to fear as she realized what might have just happened. They could have taken those guys, but how many more bands were in the ruins? She hadn't even thought that far ahead.

Hannah didn't have long to mull it over before the radios crackled: "Snow-shoes this is Blizzard, hehe. I've got twenty minutes of fuel for loitering, here. Time to get a move on."

"How about the fun part?"

"Miniguns go, Mighty Mouse go, *hyuck.*"

"Music to my ears. Stick around."

"Silent as the Night, Buddy."

O'cleary rolled to face Hannah. "Time's a wasting, girl. Let's do this."

She plotted their path through the depths of the ruins, hoping to avoid any more mobs in the labyrinth. They passed by the brilliant blue and gold gates — a reproduction Hannah knew — but impressive nonetheless. Ancient stone rose up around the team as they entered the timeworn city, robbing them of any remaining sunlight. They group pulled down their night vision monocles and pressed forward.

The first unfortunate soul in their path was a young man relieving himself near a faded iron gate. Three quick taps from Barros' suppressed weapon and the drizzle ceased. *So much for preservation of life,* Hannah thought. They bypassed other groups without raising suspicion. Hannah dared hope that they would reach the palace grounds without tipping anyone off. Her overconfidence was for naught as they saw a glow and heard the distinct sound of hammering up ahead.

Peeking around the corner, Hannah saw a man swinging a sledgehammer into the base of a statue. Another squatted in the dirt, rifling through fallen stone. Chunks already littered the ground, a testament to the skill of its destroyers. O'cleary raised his rifle slowly, looking over his shoulder for approval. Before Hannah could nod, Jenni whispered, "Let me."

The first look of genuine surprise crossed O'cleary's face.

"No chance. You're here to yap, not kill. Do yah even know the first thing about—" Before he could finish, the teenager was past him. A long, slender knife gleamed greedily in the firelight. Jenni closed the distance in two quick strides. The crouched man looked up just in time to catch the blade in his throat. He gurgled as blood poured from his severed artery. The second man reached back for another swing, unaware of the danger.

With one swift motion, the girl withdrew her steel, reached around the man, and buried the blade in his chest. He slid to the ground struggling briefly as his life drained onto the sand. Jenni gently rested the hammer on the ground. And bent over the man. "*Rayaayi khob*," she seethed.

"Sweet mother o'Mary."

"*Dios Mio.*"

The trio broke from cover and crept to Jenni's side. She turned to meet their gazes with fury in her eyes. Jenni wiped the blade on her pant leg and sheathed it. At her companions' expectant looks, she caved:

"These men are looters and defilers. This ground was old before Baghdad was a gleam in its founder's eyes. In these streets, water ran to gardens in which the very idea of law was created.

"These *men,*" she spat the words, "have no right to ravage it. They will get no mercy from me. I will leave the bodies here to rot without a *dakhma*, and this city will forget them, like so many empires before and so many it will yet."

A moment lapsed. Hannah swore for a fraction of a second that she heard the tittering of laughter on the breeze. While she still processed the gravity of the statement, Manuel checked the path ahead and gave Jenni a wide berth. They could see the palace atop the hill now: Its gardens were deserted, but figures moved along the stairs. The massive doors were thrown wide and lights danced inside the great hall. The looting, it seemed, was in full swing. Hannah surveyed the scene before turning to the others. This was already the most intense few minutes of her life, and it had barely begun.

"Around," said Manuel.

"Through," said Jenni and Brandon. Hannah sighed and made her decision. There would be no more time to waste. She unzipped her admin pouch and read from the laminated chart into her radio, "Blizzard this is Snowshoe Actual, prepare to copy."

"Ahem, standing by, Actual."

"Palace complex front steps, militia in the open. Friendlies three hundred meters east on my strobe. Make us a hole but spare the roses."

Ian echoed the command. Hannah looked at her team. All eyes were on her.

"Dad always says that close air support covers a multitude of sins." Barros laughed. "He'd be proud to see it. Let's get ready." A minute later, they heard the whine of rotors. The looters heard it too, but failed to grasp the gravity of the situation. Just as the more savvy began to move for cover, hell came knocking. Hannah went to the flat range plenty of times in the lead up to the invasion. With the government taps flowing, all mercs got hands-on experience with every weapon system they asked for.

Nothing prepared her for this.

The sky ignited with the full force of the Huey's dual M134 miniguns. Fire lashed from the rotating barrels as Ian poured unrelenting devastation onto the enemy at six thousand rounds per minute. Like a mythical dragon, it belched flames as the tracer rounds raked the entrance to the dictator's summer home. It was so bright she was forced to flip her night vision away to avoid being blinded.

Men outside ceased to exist. Chucks of masonry flew like dervishes, whirling and smashing into anyone who survived the initial strike. The pilot hosed the driveway and rooftops for good measure, powering down after less than half a minute of action. Nothing remained.

The chopper banked forward and cleared the roof, flying low over the river to prepare another pass. Hannah called him off. The man almost sounded disappointed. The occasional groan or movement drew pairs of follow up shots from O'cleary and Barros. Jenni hung back with Hannah, observing the results with a sickening grin. They reached the doors without incident, and made entry.

Boots stepped over broken glass and kicked discarded furniture. The hall was massive, a testament to the ego of its owner. The gun run meant that no opposition laid for them in wait.

O'cleary peered into the next room before lowering his guard. "Cretins were hauling out anything not bolted down. At least someone might enjoy this gaudy nonsense." "If I was actionable intelligence on the whereabouts of a despot with a chemical arsenal, where would I hide?"

"If it were you, a whorehouse in Belfast," replied Jenni.

He wheeled around. "Oh, the little demon has jokes to go with her blood-lust. Go on, do your job and look around!"

Jenni busied herself digging through scraps of papers and signage strewn about the room. Hannah checked her watch. *Ten minutes for the bird, this is taking a while.* She joined the men, trying to make sense of a large relief depicting some ancient battle; an army in triumph trampling its foes under chariots. The victorious commander looked strikingly familiar.

"Did this asshole...?"

"Hate Saddam if you want, the man knows how to make a point," said Manuel. "Put his face on everything." At that moment Jenni whistled.

"Found it. The Special Republican Guard has a panic room in the basement. Let's hit it and get the hell out."

The team quickly found stairs to the sublevels, moving quietly to avoid any ambush. At the bottom, they heard voices. Hannah raised three fingers and counted down. The mercenaries burst into the room. Inside, half a dozen men pried at a pair of large metal doors. Their Kalashnikovs were at arms length — too far.

"*La tataharak!*" Jenni yelled and motioned for them to raise their hands. "'Ana 'amzah. Alwaqt lilmawt," she stated more calmly. The men reached for their rifles. Barros put two rounds in the leftmost man's chest and a burst into his neighbor's face. O'cleary cut a pair in half with his own heavy trigger squeeze. Hannah didn't hesitate this time. Through the night vision, like hundreds of green silhouettes before them, the man in the center fell flat.

"First time?" asked Brandon. Hannah nodded slowly.

"Beers are on me then. This is the easy part. It's the remembering that gets you. Now, let's bust this open."

Manuel produced a block of plastic explosives and went to work. The others took cover in the stairwell. One loud boom later, and the doors lay open.

As the dust settled, the operators entered the room, weapons high. Inside was still. Jenni found a lightswitch and warned the others. NVDs came up just before the fluorescent bulbs. The team blinked, then stared, then looked at each other. The room was filled with gold. Bar after bar lay in neat rows piled to Hannah's chest. Each one was inscribed with Arabic writing, symbols of the Iraqi government, and Saddam Hussain himself.

Hannah's tongue practically lolled out of her mouth. There had to be tens of millions, no, hundreds of millions of dollars in metal in this room. More than she felt she could spend in a lifetime.

"How did those CIA dorks miss all this action?"

"We're gonna need a bigger bird," said Jenni. They were interrupted by a scratchy radio call:

"Snowshoe, you've got a five-truck convoy incoming and I have to head back in two mike's. Get the heck out of there!"

Hannah looked at the others. This was big — bigger than she ever expected or wanted for her first real mission. This was a life changing amount of money. Enough to keep SNW up to its eyeballs in cash for decades. They couldn't just leave it here for the scavengers.

Barros nodded like he possessed a direct line to her thoughts. "Boss, we gotta get all this outta here. We need the biggest plane we have by the border to haul ass out here. We can take care of the riff raff."

"It's a huge risk, and there are only four of us. If anyone wants out, go now." No one even flinched. *Here goes nothing.*

"Blizzard, give those trucks all you've got in the pods and bail. Get back as soon as you can and bring us a way to haul a whole load of cargo."

Ian cleared his throat: "Heh, uh yeah, sure boss, heh. Right on it. These trucks got a lot of guys and some DshKs. I'll pour it on and *vamos*. Good luck, Blizzard out!"

They raced to the main floor, hoping to find some cover for the inevitable attack. Jenni found access to the rooftop, and they took the ladder three rungs at a time. On the roof, they found the smeared remains of several people, but most importantly, machine guns and grenade launchers.

"Poor bastards couldn't kill us on the way in, don't think they'll mind us borrowing these!" O'cleary recovered a Soviet era sniper rifle, and Jenni took up a position next to him with binoculars. As they got set, the chopper came into view flying low from the north over the river. It was smoking. Ian's chipper voice came across the net first:

"Just a flesh wound up here, heh, got all but two trucks, maybe a dozen guys or so left. SRG for sure. Orange triangles and fighting spirit headed your way."

"Thank you and be safe," Hannah responded. As their protector banked hard for allied lines, the first of the enemy appeared on the road next the river. The transport trucks were barreling toward them. To Hannah's left, O'cleary whistled a low tune. She half recognized the beats. A hymn, perhaps? No time to debate. Manuel shouldered the RPG-7 and waited. Two hundred meters. One hundred meters. He looked over to Hannah. She nodded.

The rocket streaked from the roof straight down the road. The back blast threw debris and tiles across the whole roof. A second before impact, a round from Brandon's weapon decapitated the lead driver. The warhead impacted the cabin and flung the vehicle up into the air, tossing the unfortunate passengers to their deaths. The bed flipped, hung in the air, and fell into the Euphrates.

Cheers from the company were short-lived, as the final truck screeched to a halt and turned its machine gun on the palace. The much-reduced cover of the masonry was torn apart by sustained fire. They slithered to the ladder and retreated inside.

O'cleary cleared his throat dramatically. "Well, now that we have their attention, what now!? They don't seem dissuaded."

"We do what we do best," said Barros. "Disappear."

They found cover among the remaining furniture. The men locked down the front, while Jenni and Hannah watched the sides. It didn't take long. The first few men to enter were snuffed out by the suppressed rifles. The soldiers who followed poured a hail of bullets into the grand room, splintering furniture.

Barros swore as a stray round hit his foot.

O'cleary caught a ricochet in the back plate, and a glancing blow nearly knocked his helmet away.

The enemy pressed in. All sense of time left her. The force of numbers and fire superiority squeezed the mercenaries. Jenni fired a burst from a bent and bloody AK while Hannah reloaded.

Not good. Not good at all, she thought. The sustained fighting was taking its toll on her mentally and physically. Her body ached and her mouth burned. Their reloads were getting slower, and there were only a few more magazines before she also became a scavenger. Something needed to change, fast.

A soldier appeared across the room behind her. Not a good angle. He fired. Jenni ducked, and Hannah brought her sidearm up in a snap, landing a trio of hits to his torso and a fourth to his head. Her arm caught fire and red bloomed over her left sleeve.

Well, that's it I guess. First mission and I'm going to bite it and take my whole team with me. For what, some gold? What would dad say? She wasn't sure she maintained the capacity to conjure up even a disappointed facsimile of the man.

She peaked back at her men. O'cleary hefted a grenade through the open windows and braced for the blast. Manuel dropped to the ground and fired from his right side, catching his would-be killer in the legs and side with his pistol. Jenni drew her knife.

O'cleary's grenade detonated and the room shook. The foundation itself groaned, and did not stop shaking far after the shockwave should have passed. *What the hell?* That sentiment was catching on. Both attackers and mercenaries stopped shooting as the rumbling grew stronger.

"Earthquake," Jenni yelled. "We have to go!" Hannah didn't move

She didn't acknowledge the teenager. A strong, persistent thought permeated her entire psyche: *remain.* Hannah grabbed Jenni and held her to the wall.

"Stay here, we'll make it!"

"You're crazy, sister. I don't trust this palace as far as I can throw it!"

"Then trust me!"

Jenni crouched to the ground and held her hands over her head. "This better work!"

Brandon and Manuel stayed in place. Whether they received the same calming message as Hannah or were simply stuck, she didn't know.

Remain.

The ceilings cracked and soldiers screamed and fled.

Remain.

Outside in the gardens, a wall of earth rose and fell, swallowing a few desperate, fleeing men.

Remain.

The vibrations were so strong Hannah thought her teeth would rattle from her skull. She closed her eyes and hoped.

The shaking stopped. The sensation was gone.

"We alive?" she managed to choke through the dust and debris.

"Here."

"Still kicking."

"I think so, what the hell was that?" asked Barros. "Yeah, an earthquake, but this half-assed building should have tumbled, especially after what we put her through." They quickly took stock and found no hostiles. Jenni applied a tourniquet to Hannah's arm while she radioed the situation. The company managed to find an old Russian transport plane and a crazy bastard willing to fly it. How the bucket was cleared in a coalition warzone, she didn't ask. Their helicopter was almost home, ready to turn and burn with more ammo and fresh bodies. It was all over.

The team breathed a collective sigh of relief. Jenni made her way to the palace guest room for, as she called it, "additional sensitive site exploitation." Barros propped up his weapon at the door and lit a cigar. O'cleary hummed something to himself and picked at his broken armor.

As she teetered at the edge of consciousness, Hannah swore she saw a flicker of movement. She hoisted her weapon and scanned the riverbank. Whatever it was, it was small — a child, or an animal, perhaps. As soon as she focused on it, it melted away into the reeds of the bank. *Must be losing it. Time for a quick rest.*

As she succumbed to sleep, she thought, just for a moment, that she heard laughter on the breeze. The same laughter from the labyrinth. She closed her eyes and gave into sleep, leaving fantasies for the realm of dreams.

+— BONUS —+

PARAGON EXORDIUM SNEAK PEAK

The Earth shook, and the sky screamed. Evelyn tore through the living room, scooping up five-year-old Sally and throwing them both under the thick mahogany dining room table.

It had been just an ordinary Saturday; Evelyn had canceled plans with friends to see a movie to make a few extra dollars babysitting Sally.

Sally had been quiet all morning, peacefully playing with her action figures. Then, minutes before the babysitter could get up to make peanut butter and jelly sandwiches, there was a sky-splitting explosion. An explosion so loud and powerful that neither girl could hear their own screams or the crashing of pictures and furniture as the whole building shuddered.

Finally, when her eyes were now dry of tears, the quaking ceased.

"Shh... Hush now, sweetie. It's all right. We're okay. Hush now. Shhh... We're okay," whispered the babysitter to the sobbing child. After a few minutes, the sobs stopped.

Then the screaming began.

More explosions, but nowhere near the volume of the first one. The screech of tires. Gunfire, near and far. But worst of all was the silent absence of sirens. There should have been firetrucks, ambulances, police cars. The city had upgraded all their vehicles in some sort of major business deal, after all. She could not remember the details, but she remembered her parents talking about it. But there were no sirens — only the bone-chilling cacophony of panic.

The babysitter held the power button on her phone down for the fifth time, hoping maybe, just maybe, this time it would turn on.

It had been fine before; charged enough. She never let it go below fifty percent. Never. Tears running down her face, she hurled it out from under the table in a burst of rage. The phone's case protected it but not the drywall, which it dented. Sally flinched in her lap. That was when she noticed the beeping. Half the appliances in the house were beeping, as if they had all been reset.

"I want mommy," Sally whispered weakly.

"Stay here, sweetie. It'll be all right. I'll be right back," Evelyn said as she picked up the little girl from her lap. Sally shook her head with all the violent tenacity of a child, and Evelyn saw tears welling in her eyes. Then she spied a solution. A stuffed rabbit named Basil lay on the floor at the edge of the table.

She must have left him on the table after breakfast.

Sally's babysitter reached out, pulled the floppy brown rabbit to her, and then handed it to the whimpering little girl. Sally took Basil eagerly in her arms, clutching the toy so tightly the babysitter feared she would either hurt herself or break the rabbit. Evelyn could hear her whispering softly to the rabbit as she got out from under the table.

"It's okay, Basil. I'll protect you. Don't cry."

A lump formed in Evelyn's throat as she dashed over to a window. Pulling aside the purple curtains, she saw in the reflection that her auburn hair was an absolute mess.

Click. The lock on the window turned with some effort. The window itself slid open easily. She was surprised it was still intact given the volume of the noise that had accompanied the shaking.

Outside the window, the world was ending. The sounds of the city losing its collective mind filled her with dread as she looked out over it from the third-floor apartment. People were running around wildly below her, some trying to start cars, others trying to get inside different buildings. She saw what looked like a group of filthy homeless men chasing a man down an alley with large knives.

To her relief, the sky was not full of planes or parachuting invaders. *Just strange shining clouds — no, those aren't clouds. They look more like... cracks.* Her focus shifted to the smoke. Lots of smoke rising from all over the city. *What do I do?*

Something else caught her eye. There was a plane; a jumbo passenger jet. But it was not flying peacefully overhead. It was crashing, careening closer to the earth. Closer to downtown. Or what used to be downtown. She could see from the window unfamiliar white stone buildings overlapped with the usual jumble of businesses and skyscrapers, several of which were missing. *That doesn't make sense. How could there be new buildings? Am I hallucinating?*

Evelyn cursed — quietly so the little girl would not overhear. It was all too much. The panicking. The crashing planes. The random new structures. The homeless men with big knives.

Making her way back to the kitchen, she checked under the table. Sally had fallen asleep, Basil clutched in her arms. *She'll be safe here for now, I hope.* She thought as the sounds of chaos still echoed around them. Before leaving her there, she made sure the back door of the apartment was locked, then ventured into Sally's father's study. Opening the closet door, she found what she was looking for: a safe. The safe was on a high shelf well out of reach of Sally's small, prying hands.

Unfortunately, this also meant it was too high for Evelyn, since she was barely over five feet tall. With no other recourse, she clambered onto a wobbly office chair and snatched up the safe before she could lose her balance.

Once balanced on her own two feet, she turned the safe over and saw the thumbprint scanner and number pad. *Thumbprint first, then Sally's birthday backward.* Sally's father had taught her the first time she babysat.

"Just in case. You never know," he had told her with a reassuring pat on the shoulder. The safe clicked open without issue, showing her what she had come looking for, a pistol. "It's always loaded, so be sure to only point it at something if you're trying to kill it." The salt-and-pepper bearded man had said.

Evelyn tried desperately to get her phone to turn on, but no combination of buttons or chargers worked. She scrambled over and tried her laptop and then Sally's mother's desktop; none of which even flickered. *Nothing to do but wait; going outside is not an option. I'll make sandwiches. I'm not hungry, but Sally loves PB and Js. The best thing for her is to pretend everything is normal.* She was opening the peanut butter jar when she heard movement under the table.

"Miss Ev?" The young girl's voice wilted up from below.

"I'm here. Are you hungry?" *Of course, she's hungry. She's always hungry.*

"M-hmm," came the weak reply, still from beneath the table.

"Do you want to take a seat at the table like a big girl?"

She shook her head. "Do you want to stay under the table to eat?"

"M-hmm."

The simple noise brought tears to Evelyn's eyes. There was fear in that sound. She could not blame her. She wanted to get back below the table and stay there herself.

"Okay, Sal, we'll eat under the table. That sounds like fun." A few moments passed in silence while she worked on the sandwiches.

"Where are Mommy and Daddy?"

The question pulled her heart into her stomach. She had hoped the food would be enough of a distraction, but this had been inevitable.

"I'm sure they'll be home soon, sweetie." She tried to hide the fear in her own voice as best as she could. For all she knew, they weren't coming home at all.

"Can you call them?" It was a perfectly reasonable request for a child in her position, but that did not make it any easier.

"I tried to Sal, but the phone isn't working."

Silence.

She waited.

More silence from the girl, but Evelyn thought she heard screaming from inside their building. She joined the girl under the table, handing her a plate with one and a half PB and Js. One for the girl; one for her bunny.

Sally took a bite, holding back tears as she chewed. Halfway through the snack, she asked another question. "Is this a nine-eleven? Pop-pop talks about nine-eleven a lot."

Evelyn did not have a chance to answer. The screaming inside the apartment complex grew louder, joined by gunfire. Then, there came three loud, heavy knocks at the door.

Sally's eyes went big. "Daddy?" Before Evelyn could move, the little girl had dashed out from under the table, running for the door.

Why would her parents knock? They have keys. Oh, no.

"Sally, no!"

But it was too late. The girl's size had made her escape from the table much quicker than Evelyn's. The lock was undone. The door was slowly swinging open but still too fast for her to stop it. Cruel, clawed fingers wrapped around the edge of the frame, pushing the door so it slammed open against the wall.

For a moment, Evelyn thought she was looking at the devil himself. An enormous leathery skinned being who looked green in the unlit hallway stood in the doorway. He wore a strange patchwork of rags over his body and held an abnormally long machete in one hand.

No. A sword, she realized. *Whatever that is, it is not human.* The creature smiled down at Sally — a cruel expression full of rows of bloody, sharp teeth. But it was the eyes of the being that filled Evelyn with the most fear. They were yellow, the same shade you would see on a notepad, the color splintered with red irritation. There was no white in those eyes; only black pupils in a sea of burning yellow.

There was a savage glee in those eyes as they looked hungrily over Evelyn and the little girl. Evelyn's gaze was drawn to the sword in his hand, her mind focusing on the bright red blood dripping from it rather than its bizarre presence.

"You're not Daddy," Sally said in a puzzled voice, temporarily free of the mounting horror seizing Evelyn's chest.

CONTINUED IN

PARAGON EXORDIUM

BOOK 1 OF
The Galvorn Saga

linktr.ee/mikelmelwasul

THANK YOU FOR READING!

Every page read helps! But so do reviews! If you liked, loved, or hated this book please leave a review wherever possible! Amazon, Audible, Etsy, Goodreads, all help! And if you want to post anything on social media about the book we find most of our readers that way! Don't hesitate to tag Mikel Melwasul regardless of how much you liked or disliked what you read. We want to hear from you and learn how we can improve our story in future novels.

If you enjoyed this, you'll love our main series books which have some overlapping characters: The Galvorn Saga. Book One; *Paragon Exordium* is available in all formats including audiobook on audible! Book two of The Galvorn Saga; *Paragon Attrition* is coming soon!

If you liked *The Crossing*, it's an excerpt from our southern-gothic horror novella that reveals what happened to Lt. Rory from *Exordium; Paragon Odyssey!*

If you enjoyed this, you may enjoy some other works by indie authors! Check out:

The Song Of Thyssia by S.J. Stiles
Corrupted Tides by S.M. Campbell
Flipside by Leumas Llewtnac
The Wingbreaker by Megan G. Mossgrove
The Adventures of Hemera Nyx in The Galaxy of the Future! By RSK
Remnant by K.R. Solberg & C.R. Jacobson
Armitage by Atlas Creed
Voices of the Void by Patrick Leitzen
The Shards of Etherious - Arisen by Colin JD Crooks
The Guardian's Speaker Series by Katherine E. Wibell
The Apex Cycle by M.T. Zimny

Or if you want more suggestions reach out to us at mikelmelwasul@gmail.com or visit www.melwasul.com for news and signed copies!

ACKNOWLEDGMENTS

Patrick Leitzen's *Voices of the Void* Si-fi short story collection was what first inspired me to try my hand at short story format story telling. It's very different but I have thoroughly enjoyed it and hope to do more short stories in the near future. None of this would be possible if not for the encouragement and corrections from my wonderful wife Morgan, my dear friend Blake, or my co-author, editor, and general partner in crime Dave. (Who will be adding his own bit to this I'm sure). Additionally, thanks again K.R. for helping to make this pretty and keep the printing cost down even if it wasn't nearly as high this time. Lastly, a general shout out to the authors in the Galvorn Saga discord who volunteered to beta/alpha read not only this, but Attrition and for looking at my dozens of versions of the cover. May each of you walk under the bluest skies.

- M

ABOUT THE AUTHORS

Mikel David Melwasul does not exist. He is the amalgamation of the minds of three-ish individuals who conspired to write together. If you encounter him in the wild, that is most likely his "avatar" "Mik" whose body he "shares". There's also a chance it's "Dave" who he pilots less often.

If you encounter them both at the same time, run.

ARTWORK OF THE GALVORD SAGA

Captain Peter Blair by Yorsy Hernandez

Súmeriel Almurë by Yorsy Hernandez

Jadis (Isilmë Kothari) by Yorsy Hernandez

VISIT US ONLINE

Official website:

melwasul.com

Socials and book retailers:

linktr.ee/mikelmelwasul

www.ingramcontent.com/pod-product-compliance
Lightning Source LLC
Chambersburg PA
CBHW011436170626
46808CB00010B/3188